Denise M. Colby creates such warm personalities who draw you in and keep you invested in their stories. If you love Misty M. Beller and Mary Connealy, you need to be reading Denise M. Colby too!

—READING IS MY SUPER POWER

In *A Slight Change of Plans*, Denise M. Colby weaves a tender and hopeful story of second chances, resilience, and quiet courage. A beautiful balance of romance, faith, and a touch of mystery, this story reminds us that sometimes life's detours lead us exactly where we're meant to be.

—KIMBERLY KEAGAN, AUTHOR
OF *PERFECT* AND *HEART OF HOPE*

With a cast of characters sure to steal your heart (including a rooster who steals the show!), *When Plans Go Awry* beautifully touches that deep need within all of us to be loved and accepted. This deeply layered story also reveals a truth we often forget—that innate desire to trust when life has proven to be untrustworthy.

—CHAUTONA HAVIG, *USA TODAY*
BESTSELLING AUTHOR

Best-laid Plans✦Prequel Novella

No Plan at All

DENISE M. COLBY

Scrivenings
PRESS
Quench your thirst for story.
www.ScriveningsPress.com

Published by Scrivenings Press LLC
15 Lucky Lane
Morrilton, Arkansas 72110
https://ScriveningsPress.com

Printed in the United States of America

Paperback ISBN 978-1-64917-547-2
eBook ISBN 978-1-64917-548-9

Editors: Ann Harrison and Suzie Waltner

Cover by Linda Fulkerson, www.bookmarketinggraphics.com

All characters are fictional, and any resemblance to real people, either factual or historical, is purely coincidental.

Unless otherwise noted, scriptures are taken from the KING JAMES VERSION (KJV): KING JAMES VERSION, public domain.

To my writing critique group partners Marie Wells Coutu, Kimberly Keagan, and Christina Rich. This book would not have been written without your insight and thoughtful suggestions. I'm blessed by your friendship.

And for Ken. We may not always have a plan, but God has beautifully provided a life with you I love.

But the plans of the Lord stand firm forever, the purposes of his heart through all generations.
Psalm 33:11 (NIV)

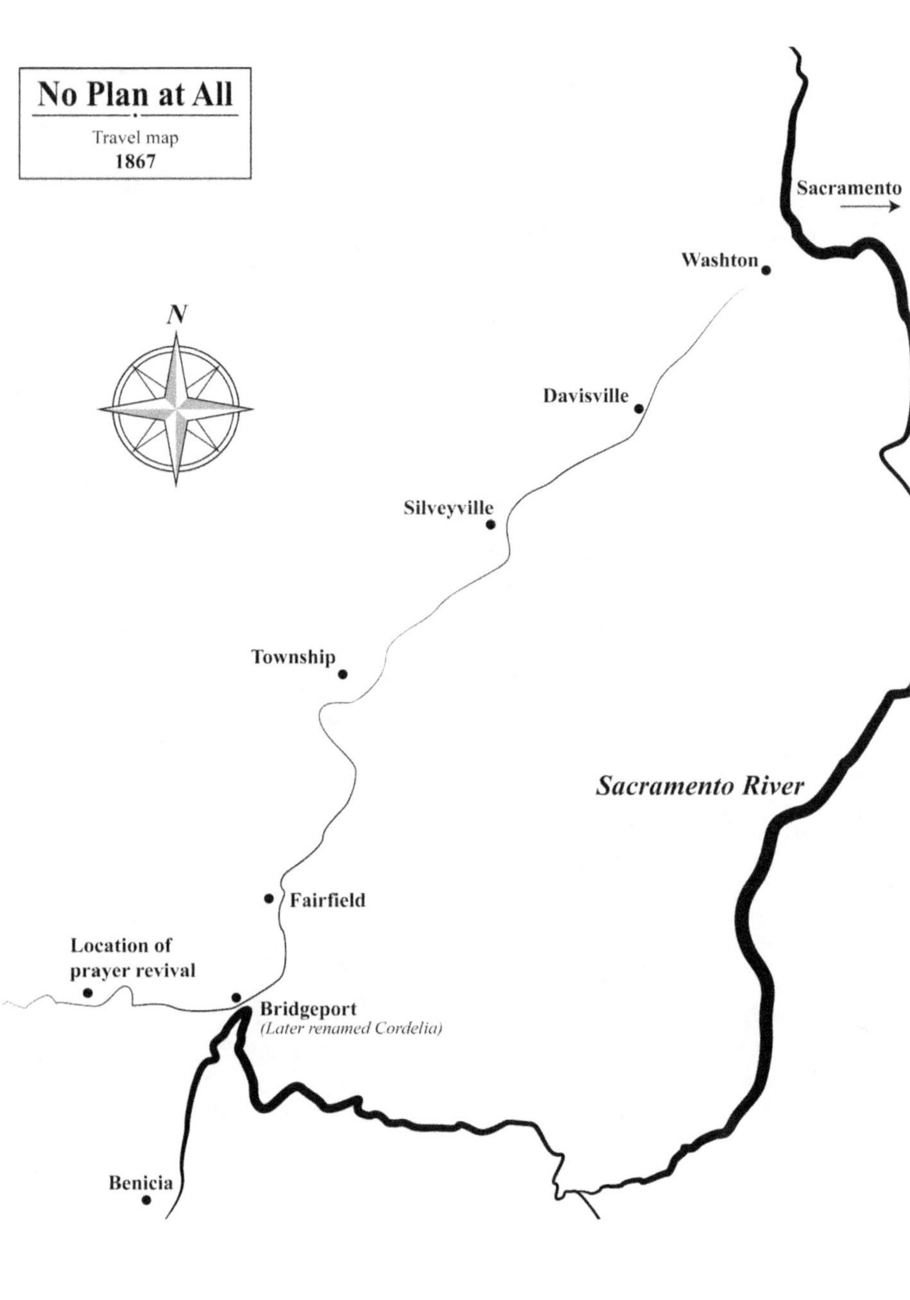

No Plan at All
Travel map
1867
N
Sacramento
Washton
Davisville
Silveyville
Township
Sacramento River
Fairfield
Location of
prayer revival
Bridgeport
(Later renamed Cordelia)
Benicia

SCOTTISH BROGUE TERMS USED:

- Och = oh
- Oot = out
- Lass/lassie = girl/woman
- Bonnie = pretty
- Aye = yes
- Nae = no
- Dae = do
- Ye = you
- Dinnae fash yourself = don't worry yourself
- Lad = boy/young man
- Aboot = about
- Whit = what
- Ah dinnae ken = I don't know
- Halo = hello
- Tak a gander = have a look
- Aye that's grand = yes, that's good

One

My annual visit to Washton is about to end. I've stocked up on all the supplies my wagon can hold. Thank you for your faithfulness, Lord, and for the people in this town. Mr. Woodward's new general store will be a great asset for this town's future. I will miss visiting this friendly community.

—From the journal of Alex Sinclair

May 16, 1867
Washton, California

Sarah Baker gripped her bag to her chest, hunching her shoulders against the downpour as her boots sank in the now-muddied ground with each step. Shrouded in darkness from the stormy night, she carried all her belongings, hoping to replace one life for another. No longer would she endure someone else's plans, living on a stinky ranch working sunup to sundown, being forced to marry her deceased fiancé's brother if she stayed.

Tears mixed with the rain. She didn't want to run away, but staying would make life unbearable. Mrs. Taylor had made it clear that Sarah and Luke must marry after she passed. And Luke agreed without ever considering what Sarah wanted. He would've jumped over the moon for his ma if she asked, dragging Sarah along with him.

She tried to explain to Luke she was still in love with his late brother, but he didn't understand. He dealt with his own raw grief of losing Michael and then his ma. Along with the full responsibility of his family's ranch and raising his two younger sisters.

Sarah wasn't anywhere near ready to take on the lifetime responsibility of a wife and mother, along with a ranch, with someone she saw as a brother only. But she couldn't stay without marrying Luke. That was plain as day. Not to mention, she'd end up stuck on the Taylor ranch forever. Ranching was not the adventure she and Michael dreamt of.

How she missed Michael. The dreams they shared. The way he held her hand for no particular reason.

She had to leave. Before things became irreversible.

Her boot stuck in the mud, and it made a loud sucking noise as she pulled it out. She continued sludging along the rain-sloshed road toward the peddler's wagon. He had shared his plans to leave, and she knew he was her only chance to escape. Tonight.

Impractical and impulsive, Sarah had a single-minded focus to save herself. And this was the best she could do at the moment. The pain of all that had happened was too much. Staying would be a constant reminder of all she'd lost.

A compulsion to look back overcame her. She squeezed her eyes shut. There was so much turmoil in her heart. From all the sickness and the loss these past six months. Staying up night after night helping them all survive. Then hearing his ma's request for them to marry and Luke's agreement without consulting her. It was all too much.

When Luke announced they would marry on the morrow, her legs went weak and she saw spots. She had told him no, but she'd never stood up to him before. He didn't believe her, and since he was as stubborn as an ox, Sarah knew he wouldn't accept her answer. Would try to wear her down.

She was so weary. Enough to have hidden her suitcase in the back of the wagon. Requested a wagon ride with Luke to town so they could talk. When he stopped, she stated her feelings, stepped out of the wagon and took all she owned, and walked away toward the Martin's, which was on her way to her destination. She'd never done something so ...

Shivering, Sarah blocked out those thoughts. Numb from both her emotions and the wet rain, she plodded onward. She had already faced Luke. Told him goodbye and to not come after her. There was no other choice but to move forward.

A faint lantern light flickered ahead, guiding her to the peddler, whose wagon sat where he'd been all week. Soon she'd leave this small town, the only one she'd ever known. Where she went, she didn't know, nor did it matter. She just needed to go.

She held her breath as she approached the covered wagon. Unsure what to do, she moved closer. But the rain drowned out any noise her feet made. Shouldn't he be outside preparing his horse? Maybe he's inside near the opening to keep from getting drenched in the downpour. Not wanting to startle him, she coughed lightly.

No response.

Her body shivered in her soaked clothes. There was no time to be subtle. "Hello," she said in a schoolroom voice.

Still no response.

Sarah expected the man who'd discussed his plan in detail

and invited anyone to join him, to poke his head out and tell her welcome aboard. Had she gotten the day wrong? Maybe he fell asleep.

Louder this time, Sarah yelled, "Mr. Smith?"

A banging came from within, causing the light to flicker from the sudden movement. A few unfamiliar words were mumbled from inside the wagon in his strange accent. "Aye, who is it?" Mr. Smith shouted.

Sarah was too cold to hesitate, even though a seed of doubt crept into her mind and planted itself. "It's me, Mr. Smith."

"Me, who?"

She blew out her breath. It was so like him to jest. He seemed a jovial person who enjoyed chatting and welcoming people to his traveling shop. "It's Sarah Baker. I'm ready to go."

Silence.

In fact, no sound could be heard anywhere as the rain stopped at that precise moment.

Panic seized her, and she slogged closer to the opening right as a head popped out between the two pieces of fabric. Sarah slunk back as she recognized Mr. Smith's golden locks, although the rain changed their appearance to a light brown. His deep blue eyes locked onto hers. When he studied her, she felt seen and heard. As if she was the most important person. He reminded her of her brother, Will. Someone she could trust.

"Och, Miss Baker? What are ye doin', lass? Shouldn't you be home asleep in ye own bed?"

Sarah frowned. "Isn't tonight Thursday? You're leaving soon, are you not? You said you planned to leave at nine o'clock. Well, it's Thursday and it's nine o'clock."

He stared at her.

She must look a fright since the rain had soaked her clothes, hair, and bonnet. As he kept staring at her, she shifted from one foot to the other. "Is there something wrong?"

He blinked. "Wrong? Aye, what could be wrong? It's raining cats and dogs, and a young bonnie lass is standing in the rain during the night telling me she's going with me. An invitation I didn't know I made. What could be wrong?"

Sarah's confidence fell. He didn't seem happy to see her. Would he not allow her to travel with him? She had risked everything on his open invitation.

A new set of tears rolled down her cheeks. Had she conjured the entire opportunity in order to find some way to escape? No. He could provide a ride for her somewhere. He had customers, which meant towns and other folks and a place to start over.

With all the bravado she could muster, she lifted her chin and searched Mr. Smith's eyes. "I need to go with you. Tonight. I can't go back. And I don't have anywhere else to go. Please. May I come along?"

* * *

Alexander Sinclair, known in these parts as the peddler Mr. Smith, stared at the terror in Miss Baker's eyes. The lass was spooked, otherwise she wouldn't be standing before him soaked with her hair drooping in her eyes like a highland cow.

She glanced over her shoulder, then back at him. "I promise I won't cause you any trouble or be in your way."

The movement wasn't lost on Alex. And the pleading in her eyes caused a knot to form in his stomach. "Have you been hurt?" He couldn't tolerate any man who used their physical strength over a woman.

Silence stretched between them, broken only by the steady patter of the rain, which started again. When she finally spoke, her voice was a whisper. "I'm okay. But if I go back, my life will be over."

The words hung in the air, heavy with unspoken fears. Alex's protective instincts flared. He couldn't say no to a lass in trouble. He'd met plenty of people out west who'd run from their homes—he was a prime example. Whatever this lass was leaving behind, it scared the wits out of her.

Despite her wide-eyed desperation and her trembling body, he'd give her points for bravery. She barely knew him, and even though California was less strict about propriety, an unmarried woman did not travel alone with an unmarried man. Whatever she was running from, she felt the risk was a better option.

"Give me a minute," he said before pulling his head back inside, where it was warm and dry.

He hadn't given her a chance to answer, but relief swept across her face.

With a heartfelt sigh, he donned a few layers of clothing, his boots, and hat. So much for a few hours of shuteye before he pulled out.

He glanced around his crowded wagon. What would he do with her? There was barely enough room even for him with all the goods he carried. Not to mention the extra supplies needed for two people would cut into what he could sell.

Alex rubbed the back of his neck. Sometimes going with the unplanned was the best course of action. He had extensive experience with adapting to new circumstances. He would figure out the details later. For now, getting her out of town before dawn seemed the wisest decision.

Would her father or any brothers search for her? Was she even of an age? And with that thought, he stuck his head out again. "Och, Miss?"

She raised her head and their eyes met. "Yes?"

"Might I ask how old ye are?" He cringed. Asking a young lady her age wasn't proper, but he needed to know.

"I'm nineteen." She answered matter-of-factly, unfazed. Her stance reminded him of a startled deer who wouldn't move when spooked.

"Aye. I'll be oot in a moment." And he pulled back inside a second time.

"Okay." Her voice quivered. "It's quite cold out here."

He wanted to tell her to get used to it because every night was cold when you didn't have a building with windows and doors to secure you. But she would realize that soon enough. The gentleman in him couldn't be rude.

He finished layering on his travel clothes and climbed out of the wagon, his boots splashing in a small puddle as he jumped down. Water sloshed onto Miss Baker's skirts, but she didn't seem to notice.

She eyed him warily as he rose to his full six-foot-two-inch frame. Taller than most men, the bulk of his arms and chest added to his size. He had his Scottish heritage to thank. Which was one reason he came out west to try his hand at hard labor, engaging both his body and mind in productive work. There wasn't much for him to do back home except play a role he wanted no part of.

He looked at Miss Baker and grabbed his hat brim. "Aye, let's load up." He stepped forward and reached for her luggage. She didn't move, only shivered, staring at her feet where water pooled around her soaked shoes. Was she succumbing to the cold already?

Grabbing hold of the handle, he pried her chilled fingers off one by one. He shoved her bag through the fabric slit on the wagon and blindly grabbed his backup overcoat and a blanket. He wrapped both around her, keeping as much space between them as possible. "Let's get you dried up first, then you can climb inside the wagon." He flicked his thumb over his shoulder.

Her eyes moved in the direction he pointed and then back to him. "You're going to let me come with you?"

"It is what you wanted, aye?"

She nodded multiple times. "Oh, yes. Please. Thank you."

He grunted. "Okay then, let's get you situated, and we can head out."

She pulled at the ends of the blanket, wrapping it further around her shoulders. "Can I ride up front with you, if you don't mind? I don't do well when I can't see where I'm going."

It would be better if she remained hidden as he drove out of town. "It's night and you won't see much."

"I won't take up much room," she pleaded. "I don't want to become unwell and have to stop."

He glanced at the sky. Great, she could retch from traveling in a wagon. "You'll continue to get wet."

"I'm already soaked. And you've given me a blanket and slicker to cover myself. I promise I'll stay quiet and hidden. No one will know who I am."

So she understood what he hadn't said.

He sighed. "Follow me." He strode to the front of the wagon and placed a hand out to offer assistance. Her cold, wet hand touched his as he lifted her into the wagon seat. He hoped she didn't catch a chill.

She settled into the far end of the wooden bench and placed his overcoat over her head and the blanket around her legs. In the darkness it would be impossible to know who she was.

But he would know. Unsure if this was the wisest move, he focused on the bridle and harness in his hands rather than the stranger in his wagon. He hadn't had a companion travel with him before. Five years of solitude and fending for himself dulled his edges. How awkward would this be?

He hoped she wasn't expecting conversation. He expended

all his energy while his shop was open, but his time afterward he spent in silence. Talking with God and his horse. Since he didn't stay in one place long, he never developed genuine relationships. Precisely why he'd come out west in the first place.

Lord, I'm not sure what you're doing here, but guide my ways. He wondered if he would regret allowing her to come along.

Two

Traveling south of Washton

Now that the initial excitement of leaving had subsided, the cold, wet weather sank in and took root, causing Sarah's bones to ache. Using the slicker as a shield, she placed her hand on her stomach, wishing it wasn't so sensitive to movement. She hadn't thought about this part. She didn't want to be a burden and have to stop frequently to settle the queasiness. Doing so would not endear her to the man next to her.

The wagon rattled slowly through yet another turn, the darkness providing the illusion they traveled in a circle, which did not help her cause. Each bend looked the same. Felt the same. Sarah had never traveled this far south before. Yet Mr. Smith seemed to know exactly where they were going. That brought about a small comfort.

Mr. Smith's gaze caught hers. "Comfortable, lass?"

Chilled, drenched, and exhausted, but she wouldn't complain. "As comfortable as I can be."

He nodded. Water fell from his hat brim. "Aye, you'll get used to it."

She smiled back, not wanting him to see her as incapable of dealing with the elements.

He faced forward again, and so did she, her eyes unable to focus on anything in the darkness. It almost made things unreal. As if she wasn't embarking on the biggest adventure of her life.

He hummed. A hymn, if she wasn't mistaken.

Happy to focus on something other than her fickle middle, the melody filtered through her mind as his deep baritone lingered on the end of the refrain. He emitted a lovely sound.

A peace enveloped her and she closed her eyes.

The wagon jerked and her eyes flew open. The quick turn caused her stomach to flip. She clung to the side of the buckboard, holding on for dear life. She had to find something to take her mind off the movement. "Thank you for the slicker. I'm not as chilled."

He glanced her way before steering the horses through a dip in the trail. "Glad to hear it. Are ye still shivering?"

"A bit. But it's better."

He nodded. An awkward silence pressed on in the darkness.

She fought to stay awake while she clung to the wagon seat under the blanket. Would it be rude to doze off? Could she even? Although sleep might ease the dizziness, she didn't want to be startled awake every so often. Her stomach wouldn't do well managing that. It wouldn't do well no matter, so she had to find a way to handle the movement. She gulped down an air bubble.

Miles passed, and the wood particles pressed into her hand as she fought for control of the contents of her dinner. She hoped not to ask to stop. But the queasiness persisted. Yawning, she wished the sun would rise so she could see. The darkness on the open trail was thick, making it difficult to know how far they had traveled from Washton.

"Whoa, Bear." Mr. Smith pulled on the reins. The wagon rocked to a halt.

Sarah sat up. "Why are we stopping?"

"Need everyone to take a break." He jumped down from the wagon and began unhooking his horse. "We're carrying a lot of weight, and it's important to stop frequently."

She let out a quiet exhale and closed her eyes, letting the relief from the stillness settle in. Did he have any idea this was what she needed?

"Dae ye want to walk around a bit?" His voice was in her right ear and she jumped, her stomach retreating from its earlier complaint. "Sorry, didn't mean to spook ye."

She willed her heart to calm again. "No, I'm okay. I'll stay right here."

"Suit yourself. We'll be off soon." He walked away. Then came back and handed her something. "Here. Eat this."

His eyes searched hers as she took the soda cracker he offered.

He had noticed.

Nibbling on the gift, she watched him reconnect his horse and climb back into his seat, causing the wagon to dip.

"Hiya."

They lurched until they moved into a steady roll.

Sarah glanced at the man sitting next to her. He was big and brawny yet refined in his manners. He settled in the wagon seat as if he had been in that position for years. His large, strong hands gripped the reins in a firm hold. Hands that could hurt someone of her size. Was she safe with him? She dismissed the thought. He'd been so gentle when he wrapped the blanket and coat around her. He acted concerned. For her. Grateful someone cared, she released her breath. After all she'd gone through, she hadn't had much time to think.

New questions arose. Where were they going? How long did he stay in one place? But she kept any questions to herself, for a smidgen of fear he would turn back if provoked. For all she knew, he was going in circles on purpose till she asked to go home.

But where was home?

She didn't have one. Not really. Not since her parents died in that awful flood five years ago. Leaving her no choice but to live with another family and work on their ranch. But then she fell in love with Michael, and they made plans to leave. Make their own way. Plans that died along with him six months ago. There hadn't been time to grieve. Not when chores beckoned, including nursing his ma who got sick soon after.

A tear slipped down her cheek. This was not what she planned. What they planned. How was everything now so different? Unfamiliar and a little frightening? She gathered the slicker around her tighter, yearning to get out of her wet clothes. But she only packed two other dresses. And since the rain kept coming, she didn't want to soak a second wardrobe.

A cold tremor flowed up her spine. Sitting this close to Mr. Smith, the man seemed much larger than when she stood in front of the wagon store he'd set up near the ferry. He had shared stories of his travels, and she had wanted to know more. Never did she think she would become a part of them.

But when things went awry over the past twenty-four hours, this was the only option she could think of. She was fortunate he agreed she could tag along.

Mr. Smith hummed another familiar hymn. "For the Beauty of the Earth." His low baritone vibrated along the wagon seat, bringing comfort to her ice-cold body. If she wasn't freezing, she'd have joined in. Anything to ignore the motion of the wagon. Although the cracker helped.

Soon Sarah's eyes drooped, the swaying of the wagon lulling her to sleep. No longer able to fight the pull, her head found a solid place to lean on, and she allowed herself to relax and rest.

* * *

THE MOMENT MISS BAKER placed her head on his shoulder, Alex forgot about the rain and the cold, forgot about the darkness, and forgot about his loneliness.

He shouldn't allow her to lean on him, but she needed rest and a break. After seeing her cringing and barely holding herself together with each turn, he pretended his horse needed a break. How did she expect to travel long distances if she suffered from wagon sickness?

His palm brushed over his day-old whiskers as he pondered the question burning in his gut. What possessed her to leave everything behind and go off traipsing around with a stranger? Was something so bad that she had to run away? And how long before she would ask to go home?

The desire for an answer to these questions surprised him. Usually, he kept his distance from anyone's personal business. Yet he wanted to know, and he didn't want to disturb her slumber, so he kept driving. Past the community called Davisville, where he would've normally rested, instead changing his plans to stop at the next town on his route. He concentrated all his energy on the muddy road until the sun's light began to peek over the rise behind them, making it easier to see problem areas.

An hour later, Miss Baker stirred. And then the pressure on his shoulder lifted. The damp chill enveloped him from where she had rested her head.

"Where are we?" she asked while pushing back the slicker and revealing disordered red hair, which had dried in all sorts of directions while she slept.

"A wee bit to Silveyville."

She furrowed her brow.

"Southwest from where we started."

She tilted her head.

He sighed. His simple answers weren't enough for her. At least he knew something about this area. "We're following the stagecoach route. The one used by the Pony Express riders when they were late for the steamboat bound for San Francisco. Silveyville was one of their stops."

She sat up a bit straighter. "Oh … I've heard of the Pony Express." She glanced around in confusion. "There's not much here."

"We haven't reached town yet."

She nodded. "Have we been traveling all night?"

"Aye, lassie." His arms could barely move.

"Aren't you tired?" She peered at him in the growing sunlight.

"Aye." He let the word linger in the stillness of the morning.

"Why didn't you stop?"

Alex looked at her. Her large green eyes stared innocently back at him. No hidden questions, no manipulation. Just pure curiosity. How could he answer this delicately? "Well, lass. I didn't think you'd be happy with me handling you while you were asleep, so I decided to keep going."

She bit her lip and turned her head away. It was obvious she hadn't thought about the fact she was alone with a grown man in the middle of nowhere.

"Thank you." She reached over and touched his arm. Warmth spread to his fingers. "Thank you for treating me with respect and being a gentleman. This may sound foolish because I barely know you, but I trust you."

Alex coughed into his hand, trying to cover the startled breath he almost let out. True, he was a gentleman in every sense of the word, but ladies did not just ride off with any gentleman without her family's consent. And if word got out now, she would surely be ruined. Although out west the rules were ever changing since women could own a business and support themselves without a husband.

"Does your family know you ran away?"

A fire lit up a fleck of gold in her pretty green eyes. "I did not run away."

He raised his right hand in surrender.

"For your information, I am old enough to make my own choices."

He'd let the topic drop, for now, but he had a right to know about her family and what might be chasing after them.

"What happens now?" She brushed at the blanket.

"Well, I'll set up my shop. While you go and see if you can find someone willing to take you in."

Her eyes widened.

"You did say you needed a ride to the next town. This is a town, although a wee one." He shrugged.

Her eyes narrowed. "How long do you plan to stay at this stop?"

"Why are ye asking?"

"What if I can't find a place, can I continue on with you? Maybe I could help in your wagon. I'm a hard worker. And I'd like to learn about what you do. Where do we get all of these items to sell? How do we replace them once we sell them?"

He pulled up on the reins. Cleared his throat. "Let's get something straight, Miss Baker."

"It's Sarah."

He glanced off in the distance and took in a deep breath. "Miss Baker. Dinnae fash yerself over my business. You're riding along for a short time, so there's no 'we' in it at all. Understand?"

She shrugged her shoulder as if she didn't believe him.

"Also, you will not need to help. Once I stop, you may go explore, shop, or whatever it is you want to do and stay away."

As he spoke, her bright, beautiful smile slowly transformed into a frown. And by George, he didn't like how that made him feel. He flicked the reins to move his horse again, his eyes searching far down the road, wishing a town would appear soon.

His protective instincts and a need to make her happy settled into his chest. He had to be rid of her and fast, before he became unable to send her away at all.

Three

—From the journal of Alex Sinclair

Sarah ignored the sting from Mr. Smith's words. He was most likely as tired, hungry, and cold as she was. Her clothes hadn't fully dried, and the combination of the crisp morning air and the damp cotton sent shivers through her. She wished for a campfire and hot coffee. Did he carry coffee? She hoped so. One cup in the morning helped her focus and gave her energy to face the day.

Energy she planned to use to show Mr. Smith how helpful she could be.

The wagon hit a rut, and they swayed in unison. The action caused her stomach to flip in a not-so-pleasant way, and she pressed her lips together. Concentrating on anything other than the motion, she glanced at him.

His chiseled jaw was set as he stared straight ahead, focused on the road before them.

She wanted desperately to ask how much longer till they stopped, but he radiated a don't-talk-with-me look. Most likely due to her use of *we*.

He glanced at her. "Whit?"

"What?" she asked.

"Yae, whit?" He nodded his head.

Sarah enjoyed the lilt of his accent, but it was difficult to understand some of his words. "I don't understand. What does whit mean?"

He stared at her a minute and a grin appeared, which then turned into a large boisterous laugh. He wiped his hand down his face.

She wasn't sure what she'd said that was so funny. Nor could she concentrate on the conversation well at the moment. She glanced at the road, trying to quell the nausea building.

"Whit means exactly what ye said. What. It's how my people say what." He pronounced the word slowly, even though his *what* still sounded like *whit*.

"Oh. Now I understand." She swung her head his way and nodded, appreciating the play on words and the thawing between them, then threw one hand over her mouth and the other over her stomach.

His eyes widened as he pulled on the reins.

She glanced everywhere in her bid to find a place to run. The motion churned her stomach further. She threw off the slicker, clung to the side of the wagon. "I have to stop. Now." Before the words were out, she jumped from the moving wagon.

"Miss Baker! Whoa."

She landed on her side. The impact halted all thought, including the reason she had leapt from the wagon. Then it appeared again. She pursed her lips together as she pushed herself to her feet. Her gaze landed on a large bush, and she ran for it. Pain radiated down her leg as she hobbled around it. But the urgency of her quest took over again and all thoughts of Mr. Smith, the wagon ride, and leaving Washton flew out of her mind as she bent over. Memories of how her mother would rub her back and hold her hair away from her face flooded her mind. Tears streamed down her face.

A few minutes later, she wiped her mouth with the back of her hand. Her body shook. She had nothing left in her system, but her stomach convulsed as it eliminated the rest of the motion sickness. She hated this part. How long it took for her to recover.

"Miss Baker? Are ye all right?" Footsteps approached the bush where she hid.

Her cheeks burned on top of her head spinning. If she didn't answer, he might see her. Her heard pounded in her ears as she pushed sound out of her mouth. "Y-yes." She swallowed multiple times, her throat sore. "Give me a second." She closed her eyes, took in a deep breath, held it, then blew it out. The dizziness subsided. She pushed herself to her knees and peeked over the bush. Her gaze collided with his across the top of the foliage.

His eyebrows were raised, but he didn't say a word.

She wanted to climb into the bush and stay there. "I-I—"

He raised his right hand. "No need to explain. You should've spoke sooner."

She shook her head, then stopped. Her body wasn't ready for much movement yet.

Mr. Smith stood straight and searched the area "I think you've chosen a good enough place for us to stop." He glanced at her over his shoulder. "Can you eat or do you need time?"

Food would help. Not knowing if she should speak or nod, she was able to produce one nod.

He clapped his hands together. "Great. I'll pull out some grub." He headed toward the wagon which was quite further down the road.

She scanned the distance from where she jumped and the wagon. As she stood, her knees wobbled like a newborn calf's. Her hip and leg hurt. She'd have a few bruises from her landing. But what else could she have done?

Once steady, she slowly limped her way to the campfire he set up.

He frowned at her leg.

She tried to hide her awkward gait but had to bite her lip to prevent expressing how much it hurt. Her hip bothered her more than she'd thought. Her vision blurred and she blinked. How would she show him her usefulness if she couldn't move well?

He patted a wooden crate. "Sit." Then he went to the wagon and tugged on a canvas sack.

She gingerly lowered her body onto the box, willing the throbbing to subside. Five minutes later, the pain subsided enough for her to glance around. Trees, dried grass, and wildflowers surrounded them. Multiple bushes were gathered in bunches on each side.

He knelt by the fireplace and opened the bag.

"Are we near the village you mentioned?" Not knowing the area was a little disconcerting.

"Aye. There's a settlement here called Silveyville I come to once a year. Now's as good a time as any to visit."

"You don't have a set itinerary you follow?"

He shook his head. "It's more a loose map. Terrain and weather play a part. Plus adding a traveling companion." He winked. "We passed Davisville, but I didn't stop there." He shrugged. "I come and go whenever I choose."

The idea of choosing her schedule, to come and go as she pleased, was the opposite of everything Sarah knew. She sighed. "Being able to come and go as you please sounds lovely."

He blinked. "Uh ... right." He produced a coffee pot and frying pan from the sack. Picking up the pot, he strode in the opposite direction of the bushes she had claimed. He went far before he bent down and scooped up something.

Now that her senses were righted, she could hear the faint trickle of water nearby. A creek. Of course they would need water.

Longing for something to do while staying put, she picked up a stick and poked the fire. She felt a little lost without a routine. And a smidgen guilty. The rest of Mr. Smith's words had finally landed in her brain and her heart stopped. She had caused him to miss one of his stops. Plus he was setting up camp in this place because of her. She was sure she wasn't helpful at all in his eyes.

Doubts stacked on top of one another, adding to the full bushel of emotions swirling in her heart as her mind replayed the events of last night. Her chest tightened. Luke and the girls appeared in her mind, and she wondered how they fared this morning. Hopefully better than she was.

She rubbed her nose. Thrust the stick farther into the fire.

Mr. Smith's feet appeared in her peripheral vision. "I think the fire has been prodded enough. Ye can brew coffee, and I'll set up camp." He handed her the filled pot.

Sarah couldn't raise her gaze to meet his eyes. She didn't have anything to hide, yet she wanted to crawl into the bush she'd found earlier. In the daylight everything was exposed.

More pronounced. The sun shone on things that were easy to hide in the dark.

How could she have been so bold to run away? To ask this stranger to take her with him. And walk away from Luke and neglect to say goodbye to the girls. Besides all those considerations, she hadn't thought through her limitations with travel. Her face, neck, and ears burned. Especially after being so light-headed earlier. She set the crock over the fire, trusting the coffee would help her mood.

Mr. Smith carried a second wooden crate from the wagon. He set it down near the fire and headed back to the wagon.

She leaned over and peeked inside the crate. It was full of foodstuffs. No longer hungry, she could at least prepare a feast for him. She stood and a pain shot through her leg. She sat and pressed all over, from her knee to hip to figure out where the pain came from.

He returned with another crate. Glanced at where her hands rubbed her leg. "Is it paining you?"

A tear dripped down her cheek and she swiped it away. Nothing was going the way it was supposed to.

He stepped closer and crouched down. "Maybe we need to find you a place to stay so you can rest. The ground is no place to be when you ache, lass. There's no way to not walk to town without my help, but maybe we can swing it. I'm assuming you have enough coin to pay for room and board?"

Sarah froze. "Um. Actually ... um ... I ..."

He narrowed his eyes. "Don't tell me you don't have any funds?"

She studied the ground, not liking her dependence on him, yet she did need his help. Besides, he'd already seen her at her worst, so she had nothing more to hide. She met his gaze. "I'm sorry, but I couldn't get any money before I left. I wouldn't steal something that wasn't mine."

He stood and placed his hands on his hips. "And pray tell, how did you expect to find a place to stay?"

From this angle, she felt small, indeed. She bit her lip. What else could she say? She'd been a guest in the Taylor home even though she had lived there for five years. They had provided for her, yet she didn't have anything of her own. The ranch needed every coin.

"Hadn't thought that far ahead, aye?" He paced, dust clouds forming around his boots.

She nodded mutely.

"I think I need some vittles in me stomach before we discuss this topic further. He knelt and cracked an egg into a small bowl. Then a second, and a third. He lifted his head. "How many eggs do ye normally eat at breakfast?"

"I don't need to eat. I'm not too hungry after ..." She waved her hand in the direction of the bush.

"I disagree. In fact, you need to eat because of ..." He pointed in the same direction.

Sarah raised her eyes to the sky.

"The Good Lord isn't going to tell you how many eggs you want." He cracked another egg. "I'll make you one. You need something, even if it's a puny amount." He vigorously stirred the eggs and poured them into the pan. Clearly, he'd been cooking breakfast in the open like this for years, which meant her cooking skills were not needed.

Would there be anything she could do to balance out the help and kindness he'd shown her? There had to be something. She just needed more time to figure out what it could be.

* * *

ALEX FOCUSED on stirring the eggs in the pan as he mulled over his options. With her injured leg, he wasn't comfortable dropping her off somewhere. She'd be a burden more than a help to anyone. His mission had been about helping people, not causing them more work.

Still, she couldn't stay with him. It was unacceptable. And even though she hadn't been coy or flirtatious, and he had no designs on her, their traveling together would be viewed as such. He couldn't protect her from the gossip.

What was he to do?

If he could stow her away inside the wagon until she was ready to go out on her own, he would. But he knew from being with her the past twelve hours she would have none of that. He was sure of it. Her affliction didn't help either.

Why couldn't he be heartless instead of a God-fearing man? Then he would've refused her last night or dumped her off at the first set of houses they'd passed.

But he wasn't made that way.

He had sisters. And a mother. He protected those who needed protecting. He observed Miss Baker from the corner of his eye. She needed looking after.

Resigned to his new fate, he shifted his attention to putting food in his belly and pulled the pan off the flames. Turning the skillet sideways he scooped a small amount into his tin. Placing a fork in the eggs, he handed the tin to his guest. "Here, lass. Eat something."

She hesitated. "Where's your plate?"

He lifted the pan. He'd eat right out of it.

She shook her head. "No. This isn't right. I shouldn't be making things more uncomfortable for you."

It was too late for that, but he kept the expression on his face the same. "It's no bother. I dae it all the time to limit the amount of dishes."

She tilted her head as if trying to figure out if he was lying.

"Here." He reached farther with the tin this time. "I'd eat before the food cools."

She stared at his offering, then reached for the tin and their hands brushed. It wasn't a caress or anything, but her soft skin was a simple reminder he had a female companion with him.

For some reason, he didn't dislike it. Which was a conundrum. He wasn't used to having another person around, yet he liked the idea of not eating a meal by himself.

He closed his eyes. *Dear Lord. Thank you for this morning. For this food, health, and your provision. Be with me in all things. Amen.*

When he opened his eyes, Alex caught Miss Baker's gaze.

She pursed her lips, nodded, then tentatively placed a small bite in her mouth. Closed her eyes. Then quickly forked some more. She *was* hungry.

Gratification filled him. Although, it helped that her lack of practiced poise made her moods easier to figure out. He bent over the pan and ate his own food, not leaving anything in the cookery. He placed the pan on the ground and reached for the coffeepot. The hot, dark-brown liquid steamed as he filled the two tin cups he culled from his inventory. After setting down the pot, he handed her one.

Miss Baker set down the tin and took the coffee. She clasped both hands around the cup and held it close to her nose. As she breathed in the aroma, her eyes drifted shut.

Alex's heart thudded and he glanced away. Scanned the area. Took a sip from his cup. Formulated a plan for the day. They were hidden a bit here, which was good, but he'd need to drive the wagon out a ways for people to see it.

"Thank you," she said.

He swiveled his head toward her. "Whit for?"

A small smile lit her face as she lifted the cup. "This. You were right. I needed something in my stomach."

His heart warmed at her words of praise. It was nice to have a little appreciation for his efforts. At least she wasn't expecting him to wait on her hand and foot. And he agreed. There was nothing like hot coffee to warm the insides on a cold brisk morning. The jolt of caffeine helped too.

Steam tickled his nose as he raised his tin to his mouth and took another gulp of the strong brew. Aye, exactly what was needed, especially after a sleepless night. Where he had to take things slower than usual. Lower visibility made it difficult to see fresh divots in the road. That's where danger lurked.

He looked to the sky. A new day was dawning, and it was time to get to work. No sense dwelling on things he couldn't change. Instead, they needed to piece together some sort of plan they both could accept.

"How's the leg, lass?" He studied her.

"Honestly, I'm not sure. It's tender but not broken. I'm sure it's fine."

He nodded. "I need to set up shop, but I'll drive the wagon a ways from camp so it can be seen clearer. You can stay here—"

"I'm not going to be left behind to sit all day long. Let me help. I'm quite good with numbers."

"Nae." He shook his head. "I have an agreement with several communities which sell me their wares at a discount. I could not slight them and let it be known that you ... that is ... "

She tilted her head. "That a woman would be doing the selling?"

Relief filled him that she'd said the words. He really didn't have an issue with it, but he knew some of the shopkeepers were extremely traditional. If they refused to sell to him, he wouldn't have enough items to make a profit. "Quite frankly, aye."

She frowned. "I'm not sure I understand. What's the problem?"

"Believe me when I say that a young lady hawking wares from one city to the next would be such a novelty, the word would spread quickly."

Miss Baker made a face that was quite comical. "I really don't want to bring attention to myself."

That made two of them.

"But I think I could be helpful in some capacity. What if you get too busy at once? I could make things go faster, or hand you items from inside the wagon. Or I could stand outside and encourage people to come check out your wares. Don't you think we could find something for me to do?" Her hopeful, bright-eyed gaze caused a lump to form in his chest.

How was he to protect her reputation when she had no idea the decisions she made could cause herself harm? How could he say nae to her eagerness? He knew one thing. If she stayed in camp on her own, she'd likely find trouble. But if she was with him, at least he could keep an eye on her.

"All right. You can come with. But you stay in the wagon the entire time. Understood?"

A grin spread across her face. "Understood. I promise I won't be a bother."

Alex hoped she could keep that promise.

Four

Today's sales were strong. At this rate I'll run out of supplies before I can replenish. Good problem to have.

—From the journal of Alex Sinclair

Sarah sat on the floor of the wagon, tucked into the back of the buckboard and hidden from view. Her leg wouldn't allow her to do much more. Both she and Mr. Smith agreed sitting outside with a bum leg would draw more attention than either of them wanted. Instead, she handed him things nearby. She also watched and learned. What she saw from this new angle provided a different perspective of Mr. Smith.

He fielded a constant stream of requests without a hint of impatience. Gave an extra piece of candy to each young child so he could carry a conversation with the frazzled mother or frustrated father. The questions he asked his customers probed in a way for him to find the exact item they required. He never suggested extra items to gain additional sales.

That baffled her. Wasn't the whole point of a wagon full of goods to make as much money as possible? Yet as the hours passed, she noticed a pattern. Mr. Smith didn't aim to sell everything—just the right thing to the right person.

He genuinely cared about each person who came to his wagon. Only offered what they needed. And when it was obvious a family couldn't afford a certain good, he lowered the price without anyone the wiser. She hadn't caught on until she saw the same item sold multiple times at different prices.

It was a new type of tin can opener. Safer and more expedient than a chisel and hammer, the tool was a novelty, and something he ensured many were able to purchase. When a mother showed all her coins in her possession, he sold it to her for exactly that amount.

Sarah found the grins from the customers as they left with their purchases contagious. The joy hearing their thank yous was something she hadn't experienced before. In her past, she was the one receiving handouts due to her circumstances. But to serve others and not need something in return? That was a new sensation.

By the end of the day his wagon supplies were half gone, which she deemed a huge success. All the money he made from this one day seemed enough to last a week.

As his last customer strode away, arms full of purchases, Mr. Smith turned to her and clapped his hands together. "Aye, a good day." He grabbed the brim of his hat and smiled.

Her lips lifted in response. "Yes, indeed. What now?"

"We pack up and head back to where we started this morning. We can pull out again after some shut eye." He stacked baskets and placed them at Sarah's feet. "How's your leg?"

Sarah frowned. "I'm not quite sure. I haven't moved all day." Which was probably a good thing. She hoped it didn't give her any more problems. Sitting all day and not doing anything was not in her nature.

He paused. Glanced around as if trying to figure something out. "I'm sure it needs some stretching. Do you mind staying where ye are until we get back to camp. I don't want to risk someone seeing ye."

She bit her lip and nodded. He was doing his best to protect her. She'd comply, even if it meant cramming herself into a stifling, enclosed space with her back to the horizon. She had to handle the minor discomfort. For both their sakes.

Mr. Smith jumped out of the back. The wagon tilted as he climbed into the seat. "Yah, Yah."

The jolt threw Sarah's head back and she gripped the wood crates on either side. Should she close her eyes or keep them open? Staring straight ahead, she focused on the scenery through the opening in the canvas. The wagon's sway turned her stomach, but she squeezed her entire body into submission. After an early turnaround, the path straightened, and she caught a small glimpse of Silveyville. The one-story buildings were spaced apart more than Washton's Main Street. But maybe that wasn't the main part of Silveyville. Or it was even smaller than what she knew.

"Whoa." The wagon stopped and dipped. Mr. Smith came into view. "How did ye fare? Want some help getting oot of there?"

His thoughtfulness about her motion-sickness was not lost on Sarah. She threw fisted hands into the air, focusing on anything but how her stomach felt. "I made it."

He laughed as she intended.

She dragged herself down the floor of the wagon bed a bit, her body stiff from being in place for too long. "Let me come to the edge and then I'll need your help to alight."

He nodded and looked away to give her privacy.

She placed her hands behind her to push and scoot further. The process was slow, but she finally made it to the edge. When she placed her legs over the ledge and leaned forward, her feet touched the ground. "Ouch."

Mr. Smith spun around and reached for her but stopped just short of touching her. His hands hovered near her arms. "Are ye okay, lass?"

Sarah closed her eyes and bit her lip. The pain subsided enough and she opened her eyes. "Yes. Give me another minute to adjust to standing."

He stepped back but watched her closely.

She gingerly lifted the sore leg and took a step. Tender, her hip throbbed but held her weight. When she stepped forward with her other leg, she couldn't help but limp. But she held her own. She pivoted to move around the wagon, away from his waiting arms. His attention and care stirred a longing she didn't think she would ever feel again.

Could she move beyond her love for Michael? She shook her head. She didn't want to. She wanted to never forget the love they felt, and the plans they'd made. But he wasn't here with her now. He never would be.

Footsteps followed her, but she focused on placing one foot in front of the other. She didn't want to fall. She didn't want to show any weakness.

"Where are ye going?"

She didn't know, but desire to move pushed her forward. "My leg needs exercise. Movement. Anything." After taking multiple steps without falling, she stopped at the flank of the horse still tethered to the wagon. "He's beautiful." Her hand raised. She spoke to the animal before touching him. "Hey, boy, can I pet you?'

"Aye. He'd like the attention." Mr. Smith stopped a respectable distance behind her. "He's ready to be tended to."

"I can do that. I assisted with the horses on the ranch. What's his name?"

"His name is Berrymin." Mr. Smith cleared his throat.

She peered into the horse's eyes. "What a peculiar name." Her fingers dug into the horse's hide, the connection between them having a calming effect. Not to mention he was something she could lean on for a moment.

Berrymin flicked his ears.

"Not really." Mr. Smith unhitched the leather strap connecting the harness to the reins. "I call him Bear."

She laughed. "Can he be a bear sometimes?"

He chuckled along with her. "When he's obstinate, I call him Lord Bear."

* * *

ALEX WINCED AT HIS MISSTEP, but relief swept through him as Miss Baker laughed.

Her laughter was catching and he joined her, while they both loved on his best friend. Better to let her believe his Lord Bear comment was a funny name for his horse than for her to find out the truth about the nickname. Her interest in his faithful companion caught him off guard, something that hadn't happened often since he set off on his own five years ago.

Saying Berrymin out loud reminded Alex of who he was and where he came from. Lord Berrymin of Bruin. He didn't plan to fully lose his identity, but here in California, titles were as worthless as pots with holes. He was Mr. Smith, peddler of wares. And he intended to keep it that way.

He grinned at Miss Baker as they continued to pet his long-time friend.

She grinned back. "Where are you from, originally?"

"Scotland." He couldn't hide his accent, and this much of himself he could share.

"That's far away from here."

"Aye." What else could he say?

"How many years have you been gone from home?" She focused on Bear's neck.

He hesitated. But it wouldn't hurt to answer in truth. "Five years."

"That's a long time. Do you miss your family?" The way she asked the question made Alex think she was wondering about her own situation.

"Aye. Sometimes." Their eyes met. "I like what I'm doing though. It's worthwhile. It gives me purpose."

Their gazes locked, and a connection passed between them. It was as if the loneliness he carried around with him had lifted. He shook off the sensation and reached for the reins. "Let's stake him for the night in the same spot as earlier." He led Bear to the patch of grass by a small copse of trees.

He didn't really worry, per se. Bear would never run off unless startled, and if he did, he would eventually come back. Alex just needed to put some space between himself and Miss Baker.

"I can help," she called out behind him. Her uneven footsteps pounded the dirt, as she tried to keep up.

Indecision warred within him. He didn't need her hurting herself further, and her determination wouldn't allow her to take care of herself. He slowed his pace so she could catch up.

It took a few moments for her to reach him, but thankfully she didn't say anything while she placed herself on the other side of Bear. Even with a bum leg, she moved around with so much energy. Free and alive.

A freedom he strived to find every day.

He peered around the small meadow. The colorful wildflowers reminded him of Scotland. Just enough of home to allow him to stay in California, away from the life where he grew up.

"Is this the spot?" She stopped and tugged on the bridle.

He blinked. So into his thoughts, he strode right by the place he wanted. "Yes, sorry. My thoughts were elsewhere." He retreated a few steps.

Miss Baker jumped right in and took charge of staking Bear. "I'm sure you're exhausted." Her movements were skilled and practiced, confirming she knew how to care for a horse.

He turned and faced the cart. "Aye. I am." The fatigue had settled in his body, and he was about to fall over. A long night of slumber was exactly what he desired. In his wagon. But he couldn't sleep inside *with* Miss Baker, and he couldn't leave her outside by herself. So a night on the ground it would be. Maybe he was tired enough his body wouldn't notice.

He sighed. How was this going to work? They should not be out here together. Alone.

Miss Baker walked up alongside him, brushing her hands together. "Bear is all staked. What's next?"

He headed to the wagon. "Next we make camp and fix supper. The wagon will block the wind. Ye can sleep by the fire. I'll take the other side."

She looked where his finger pointed and nodded. If she was nervous, she didn't show it.

He worried for her. Did she have any idea what she got herself into? And was it too late for her to go back? She must have family who would worry about her. If his sister did anything crazy like this, his father would send dozens of servants riding all over the countryside to search for her.

So where was her family? Was she all alone?

A protectiveness flared inside of him. And as much as he tried, he couldn't think of Miss Baker in the same way he thought of his sister.

Five

Sarah had not thought this far ahead.

To nighttime. Sleeping, outside, near a stranger, who happened to be a man. Her brother would have her hide. She didn't dare voice her concerns, or Mr. Smith would take her back to Washton. She had wanted an adventure. Well, here she was, right in the middle of one. It may be without Michael, and not exactly what she had in mind, but she was acquiring new experiences. She had to make the most of them.

Sarah restarted the fire while Mr. Smith brought out the bedding and foodstuffs. Since she spent all day in the wagon, she now knew he used some of his merchandise for her. Somehow she'd have to repay him. Hopefully after some rest, her leg would work properly tomorrow.

After dinner, which consisted of beans and dried meat heated over the fire, they settled in on their respective sides of the campfire pit, the flames dancing between them. Mr. Smith pulled out a guitar and started strumming. He closed his eyes and tilted his head as the notes blended into a tune. A beautiful sound filled the air, with the crackling fire providing accompaniment.

"Where did you learn how to play guitar?" she called out.

He didn't answer for a moment as if lost in the music. "You've seen one of these before?"

She nodded and then realized he couldn't see her well. "Yes. My brother has one."

"Tell me more about your brother."

She hesitated. If she told him anything, would he use it against her? Or was he asking to fill the silence? "I haven't seen him in almost two years."

"Does he write?" he asked as if not seeing your sibling for two years wasn't a big deal.

Her mind searched for the answer. "Once a month."

"Aye, that's good."

"Good? What do you mean good? He's my only living relative. And he left me. Watched out for me for years but when he turned twenty, he left us. And then there was all sorts of death, destruction by the floods, and drudgery to deal with. And he wasn't there when I needed him most."

She gulped down the cold air to calm herself. If she could've stood easily, she would've stormed away. Instead, the weight of her words settled over her, making her feel small. She hadn't realized how much hurt and sorrow had bottled up inside of her. Getting it off her chest felt good.

Mr. Smith kept strumming but said nothing.

Heat flooded her cheeks over her outburst.

"Where did he go?" He continued to finger the guitar

strings, staring at the fire. No comment on her eruption or his opinion on the matter. No words of comfort either.

She swallowed. Twice. Then hid her mouth behind her hand. "He went to seminary."

The strumming halted. "What did you say?"

Her chin quivered. "He's away at seminary."

Mr. Smith shifted the guitar to the side. "He's serving God, and you're upset with him? He chose an honorable profession, aye?

This was why she never shared her feelings with anyone. She had them and didn't know what to do with them. No one understood. "Forget I said anything." She'd stuffed down her emotions for years, she'd push them back inside again.

He strummed something off-key. "Nae, lass. It's been said. And it's here." He touched his heart. His gaze reached hers all the way across the firepit. "Festering. Impacting your relationship with God. Your ability to heal from the hurts you've experienced. You can express yourself here around the campfire and hopefully it will help."

Wait, what was he saying? Wasn't he mad? Why was he helping her, telling her that expressing herself was okay? She wiped her wet cheeks. "I-I-I do feel better. I didn't realize I had all that inside of me."

"Trauma can do that." He strummed a few more notes, then placed his hand on the strings, stopping the music abruptly. "Let me ask you something, lass. Did you think about how running away with a stranger might affect your brother or his career?"

"How would this affect his career?" Sarah's heartbeat accelerated. Was Mr. Smith on her side or not? She fisted her hands and leaned forward. "This has nothing to do with him. He isn't aware of the things I've been dealing with, nor what happens to me because he isn't here."

Mr. Smith sat there, unmoved by her passionate plea. "Och, Miss Baker, that's where you're wrong. Your brother chose that profession so he could help not only his community but you too. You do realize if word got out of you leaving in the middle of the night, unmarried, and with a man, he might not have people support him as a pastor? Who would want him to lead their flock if his own sister doesn't live in an honorable, moral way?"

"But I haven't done anything wrong. I'm not doing anything immoral."

"You know how the people of the world see things. The *perception* is much worse than the actual reality."

She stood and fisted her hands, ignoring the fire of pain shooting down her leg. "But it's so unfair. Men can go where they please, take any job they want, and no one questions them. But if a woman leaves home, she's reckless, or worse. What if we don't want to get married, or we want to choose what we do with our lives?" She shifted and limped away from the fire, dust digging into her shoe as she dragged her injured leg.

The darkness engulfed her, and she stomped her good foot. "Argh." Never had she felt so alone. Not even when she walked away from Luke last night. She'd have to figure out how to travel by herself. It was obvious Mr. Smith did not agree with her choices. As much as she wanted to run, she couldn't, and that fact churned inside her. Always stuck. With limited options.

She huffed out a breath, turned and headed back, stopping where her blanket lay. She bent, settled back down on the ground, and wrapped the thin cloth around her legs. "I'm so tired of everyone else making decisions for me."

"Aye, lass." Mr. Smith acknowledged her words, and she

calmed a bit. At least he listened and didn't chastise her further.

He strummed a few more notes, then stopped the music, staring at the flames. "Well, I may not agree with your rationale, but there is one thing we agree on."

Sarah narrowed her eyes. So far he hadn't been the comforting ear she wanted. "What's that?"

"I left my family because I was tired of everyone else making decisions for me too."

*   *   *

ALEX BROKE a piece of the grass at his feet. He hadn't meant to be so rough on Miss Baker. But her point of view was an interesting pill to swallow. Five years ago, he had stood in her shoes, spitting the same words at his father. *I'm so tired of everyone else making decisions for me.* At the time, he'd believed he was declaring his independence. Looking back, it felt more like the tantrum of a petulant, selfish young man.

Interesting how they both yearned for freedom from other's expectations. Yet Miss Baker's perspective brought to light something he'd been too young to see, or understand, before. How his leaving affected the rest of the family, including his two sisters, who were quite young when he left.

Although, at the time, what choice did he have?

His intended bride was ten when their families made the agreement. He couldn't stay and watch her grow up, then marry her and not view her as a little sister. He knew his responsibility and planned to follow through with the commitment, but he asked his father for eight years on his own before he married her. He sweetened his proposal with a promise to find and connect with other members of the Sinclair clan on the west coast and to find land to purchase.

Of course the western world was a different place. One had to claim a stake and work the land to keep it. And everyone wanted to own their own parcel, not work for someone else. Educated and raised with privilege, Alex had never been subjected to hard labor. But he wasn't afraid of backbreaking work. His body was built strong like his countrymen. But after a while, physical labor and satisfaction with the results wasn't what his heart yearned for. Maybe if he had his own land. But none of the clansmen he'd found wanted to follow that path. They were too busy panning for elusive gold.

He set out to learn and explore the area, serving people along the way. Which was how he stumbled on the peddler wagon. A much better investment in his mind.

He chuckled. He and Miss Baker did have quite a bit in common in that way. But there was more to her story, and he wanted to learn what he could. "Lass, ye said your brother's your only family. What happened to ye parents?"

"They were both killed in the flood in 1862." Her voice was barely above a whisper.

He had heard stories about the floods when he'd first arrived. Overflowing banks, fast currents, and many lives lost as well as property. "It must've been traumatic. How old were ye?"

"Fourteen," she answered in a small voice.

"Just a wee one, then. Where did ye and your brother go?"

"We moved in with my brother's best friend's family. The Taylors. Mr. Taylor died in the flood as well."

Why did every family have to endure tragedy and heartbreak?

"Was it a burden to live there?" He didn't know why he asked so many questions, but since she kept answering, he wanted to keep the conversation going. Anything to push away the silence and the awareness of them being out here, away from civilization.

"It wasn't horrible. A lot of work. Sun-up to sun-down. But the family was kind."

Did her tone get wistful? How he picked up her emotions in the dark amazed him. His senses honed in on her voice and her chosen words.

"Tell me more, lass."

"That's where I met Michael. He was handsome and funny and he let me cry on his shoulder." She clearly had feelings for Michael but talked about him in the past tense. Something must've happened to him.

"We planned to marry."

"Hold on. I thought you said everyone was pushing you to get married, but you said ..."

She sighed. "No, Michael I wanted to marry. Luke I did not."

"Wait, who's Luke?"

"Michael's brother."

"You were going to marry two brothers?"

She released a frustrated laugh. "No, silly."

He wasn't trying to be silly, but he found her joy easier to deal with than her sorrow.

She paused. "Michael got sick. His ma did everything she could, but he grew weaker and weaker until he couldn't hold on anymore."

He heard her swallow, indicating what came next was hard for her to say.

"His ma got sick shortly after Michael ... passed. Luke and I did what we could, caring for the younger girls, the ranch, and ma. She passed away on my nineteenth birthday."

Sorrow filled him. There would have been no celebration on that day.

"Before she passed, she begged Luke and me to marry. I know she did it to protect me and to help Luke form a new family with the girls, but I ... I ..."

"It wasn't what you wanted."

"No. I couldn't say anything, and Luke agreed with whatever his mom asked. I—couldn't." She threw down her hands. "I didn't want to be stuck in a marriage I never wanted. It wouldn't be fair. To any of us."

"Whit made you search me out?" Alex suspected he knew the answer, but asked anyway.

Her head lifted, and her gaze found his through the flames. "I visited your wagon last week. Heard your stories of adventure and exploring. It's what Michael and I dreamed of, and something I yearned to have for myself someday. But when Luke said we would marry right away, which would've happened today, I packed my bag, and well, you know the rest. You were my only chance to prevent this unwanted marriage."

Alex shifted on his blanket. He had believed it was more than that at the time. That she was in danger. But given what she told him, he could understand the urgency. Show grace when needed. "Whit did you tell Luke?"

A sniffle broke the quiet. Then another.

Alex tensed.

Across the fire, she sat motionless, her face turned away. She swiped her arm across her eyes.

Alex glanced at the starlit sky. *Lord, help me.* He never could handle tears. Not from his sisters, and certainly not from a woman who'd already lost so much.

The need to ease her pain urged him to stand, brush the dirt from his trousers, and walk to where she sat.

She looked up at him, wet streaks forming lines on her face.

He sat and opened his arms. "Come here, lass."

She turned into his shoulder and cried. Big, long sobs. As if she was releasing her burdens into the atmosphere.

He patted her back and offered what support he could. "You're not alone. God is with you. He never leaves you nor forsakes you. But ack it's hard to sense that he's there in the thick of it." Her story touched him. Similar to others he'd helped over the years. The reason he never saved enough money to purchase any land. Someone else's needs were greater than his.

And right now, this little snippet of a young lady had needs. Someone to take care of her. To help her gain her footing until she had some sort of plan. Not be dropped off at the nearest inn and left on her own.

Which meant she was staying. And they'd figure things out as they went along.

Everything is in disarray. My schedule. My peace of mind. My plans. What am I to do, Lord?

—From the journal of Alex Sinclair

Sarah's head fit perfectly on Mr. Smith's shoulder while his arm provided comfort she hadn't felt in a long time. She'd been with him for less than twenty-four hours, and already he'd asked her more questions than anyone had in years. Whether he was truly interested or not didn't matter. She needed to talk. To put words to her thoughts so she could organize them and figure out where she came from and what she wanted. She didn't have all the answers, but her heart said she was on the right path.

"Are you okay, lass?" His murmured words tickled her hair.

She lifted her head. "I think you should call me Sarah." He released her, and she stared into his deep blue eyes, the color of the sky after a storm blew away the clouds.

He swallowed. "Nae. Ah dinnae ken that would be proper."

"Proper?" She let out a soft laugh, motioning around their makeshift camp. "None of this is proper, Mr. Smith."

He smiled, his eyes crinkling at the corners. "Aye." He glanced out into the darkness, then back at her. "If I'm to call you Sarah, you may call me Alex."

"Alex." The name felt familiar, yet incomplete. "It's short for something?"

He looked out into the darkness again. "Alexander."

The fire crackled at the same time he answered. "What was that again?"

He shifted and faced her, placing additional space between them. "Alexander."

She smiled. "A lovely name." So many mysteries within this man. At first she thought he was a decent person, but after watching him all day, he was much more. She couldn't define it yet, but she would eventually.

He winced. "It's aboot time we get some shuteye." He pushed himself to his feet. "Good night, lass."

"Good night." Sarah was tired, but her mind replayed their conversation, putting her thoughts into some sort of order. "And Alex?"

He had made it all the way to his side of the firepit and placed another log on the fire before he glanced at her.

"Thank you." She had a lot to figure out still, but her head was clearer thanks to his compassion.

They settled in for the night, but Sarah couldn't sleep. The nighttime sounds played as if they were right next to her ear. Never had she heard the noises of the many creatures that came to life during the night. She usually hid under a warm, thick blanket indoors, nice and toasty. The fire offered enough heat to keep the chill away, and her lids grew heavy as she watched the flames dance in an uneven rhythm.

She woke to find herself in a strange place, unsure and confused.

"Good morning, Miss Baker. It's a bonnie morning, aye."

She raised herself on both elbows as Mr. Smith, no Alex, held out a cup of coffee. His accent was more pronounced this morning. Was he more comfortable with her, or did he need coffee first thing like she did?

"Ooh. Is that coffee? Much appreciated." She reached for the offered tin cup. Sipping the hot brew, her mind awoke. Along with the reality of her situation. The hard ground gave no sway last night, and her body ached. She touched her hair, hoping it didn't stand out in every direction like it did most mornings. She must look a fright. Even living with brothers, she never saw them until she'd combed her hair and dressed for the day. And she had never slept in her clothes and undergarments before. She had never run away, either, so all of this was a new experience.

Alex whistled while he worked around the camp, packing things up.

She felt lazy sitting there sipping her coffee. "Do you set up and tear down camp every day?" Sarah sat up further, testing out her hip and leg. It still pained her, but less. Hopefully, she could walk on it without limping.

"Yes, ma'am."

She bristled at his use of ma'am, as that was what the cowhands called Ma Taylor. Wasn't it decided last night they would use their first names? Was he upset with her because she slept too long? "It seems like a lot of work."

"Aye."

She watched him roll up his bedroll. She raised to her knees, placed her tin on the ground, and did the same. "Why do you do it then?"

"Do whit?"

He was distracted. As if he was putting distance between them. In some ways she was relieved, but she didn't want their interactions to be awkward.

"Why do you pack up every night? No one is around. Can't you leave things?" She stood and waited to see what her leg would do.

"That would be like inviting a'body to me stuff oot here."

"What?" She glanced at him. Maybe if she watched him speak she would comprehend what he said.

He paused what he was doing and turned. "Miss Baker."

"Sarah." She smiled at him.

He pinched his lips together. "Aye, Sarah. I'm packing up because we're moving on this morning."

She opened her mouth and closed it again. "Okay. I didn't realize that." She hugged the rolled blankets to her chest. "It would be helpful to know your plans. Then I can help."

"Ah dinnae ken—"

She held up her hand. "Please speak English. I'm having a hard time making sense of your words."

He frowned. "Sorry, lass." He placed his hands on his hips and studied the ground. "I don't know what has come over me. This." He flung his arms wide, then shook his head. "I don't have a plan. I just go with my gut. And I think we need to move oot. Now."

She nodded and took a step forward, shaking out her skirts a little. She still couldn't put all her weight on her leg, but at least her skirts would cover her limp. Hobbling over to the back of the wagon, she placed her bedroll inside. How long till the next stop? Would they be riding all day? Was she ready for that? She had so many questions but was afraid to ask.

And he didn't seem likely to answer any of them. Where had the kind and caring man who'd held her last night gone?

* * *

WHAT HAD GOTTEN INTO HIM? Alex wasn't one to be short with others. Nor become distracted enough to revert to his native language. They couldn't stay here for multiple reasons. Staying there a second night would draw attention, and the memories of their exchange lingered in his mind.

He had watched her limp less as she carried her bedding to the wagon. She was quiet and focused on loading the wagon, which he appreciated. But her glances his way every few seconds told him she had questions lurking.

She turned to face him. "Is there anything else that needs to be done?"

Smoke billowed from the fire pit as he poured the last of the coffeepot over the flames. The puff cloud sent ashes into the air and near his boots. He backed up a step but watched the steam until he was sure the fire was out.

He swung around, the last of the pots and pans hanging from his hands. "I think that's it. Just need to put these away and harness Bear."

The mention of his horse reminded him of their conversation from yesterday. Something he was trying hard to forget. He appreciated her sharing her history with him. He'd asked. And now that he knew she'd had it rough, his nurturing side wanted to protect her. He had left his family, but they were still alive. She lost hers. Including the man she planned to marry. He had no room to complain. About anything.

It was natural for her to be upset and need a shoulder to cry on. Sometimes that was all anyone needed. But when hearts were bared and hurts acknowledged an invisible string connected people. It was that connection he tried to push from his mind. He had hoped last night's conversation wouldn't make things uncomfortable. But his mind wandered to the comfort part, and somehow the wall he'd erected wasn't tall or thick enough. And he couldn't allow any feelings to develop.

He placed the pots in the back of the wagon and brushed the dirt off his hands. "Everything's ready to go."

"We travel a ways down the road and then do everything all over again?" she asked.

He nodded. "It seems repetitive, but nae, it's not." Move forward to the next stop. To the next set of people. Don't stay in one place too long. Surface relationships, limited interaction. This was his life. Or was it? Having Miss Baker along was a new occurrence, and he wasn't sure how to manage it.

Bear lifted his head from the grass he ate as Alex approached.

"Sure you don't want my help?" Sarah stood at the back of the wagon holding on to the side.

"Nae. Wait for me at the wagon bench, and I'll help you alight after I connect him," he called over his shoulder. "Ready for another day of travel, boy?" The reins dangled as he led his horse to the wagon. "It will be lighter today." He glanced at the sky. "No rain either."

Alex focused on connecting the harness before he offered a treat to his friend. When he glanced up, Miss Baker already sat on the bench seat. Squished to the far side as much as possible. His lips lifted at the corners. He was so used to people following his commands, he wasn't sure how to respond. From the moment she arrived she did things her own way. He sort of admired her for that. *Sort of* being a key part of that thought.

He climbed onto his side of the small bench seat and picked up the reins.

"How far are we traveling today?" Her hand gripped the side of the wagon as he signaled for Bear to move out. He was learning her tells. Before he thought she wanted to know details just to know them. Possibly to question his authority. But with her sensitive nature to the rocking of the wagon, he'd discovered she was managing her body's reaction.

He didn't have anything specific but could provide information about the next town. "To Vacaville Township. It will take us all day. Eleven miles."

Her body swayed with the wagon, and she kept her eyes focused forward. "What will happen there?"

"I'll restock with fresh foods and goods. The train brings refrigerated cars to their depot."

"All day?" She glanced his way.

He chuckled. "I do hope to stop along the way and sell what I can."

Her shoulders sagged in relief. "Can I help this time?"

"Nae."

"I don't think anyone will care. You don't need to protect me. My reputation back home is already ruined."

Her fiery spirit he *did* admire. But he wouldn't budge on this. "I care." Not wanting that to be misconstrued, he added, "Maybe I'm trying to protect meself too." He paused. The truth of his words landed hard in his chest. "We can do what we did yesterday, aye. You sit inside the wagon. Help behind the scenes."

She bit her lip as she faced forward. But he knew the discussion wasn't over.

Not once had someone challenged him so freely. Yet her questions exposed himself, his motives, and his actions. If he wasn't careful, she would get under his skin. He could easily discount it, because she reminded him of his sisters. Yet he related to her in a different way. What she shared last night was too much the truth of his situation as well.

He'd always thought he was alone in wanting more. In craving a life beyond obligations and expectations.

To find someone who desired the same lit a flame in his heart. A yearning. Yes, he'd had more freedom than she did. He was living on his own, exploring new places. But there was still a halter on him and after five years, it felt tighter than when he had begun.

And now he knew why. His time was running out.

After several miles, they came across two young boys running down the path.

Alex waved.

They waved back and changed direction. Hopefully to announce his arrival. That was how word usually spread when he was in town.

He pulled over and pointed to the location he planned to stop. "See those bushes and trees? They will provide privacy and shade. We'll stop here for a few hours."

Sarah jumped down as soon as he pulled on the reins.

As she walked over to the bushes, Alex unharnessed Bear. "That was a gentle stroll for you, wasn't it boy? You did good. We'll have to travel that way while Miss Baker is a guest with us. But you don't mind, do you? You like the extra attention she provides." Alex did too. And that worried him.

Without a word, Sarah climbed into the back of the wagon and stacked crates in the same order he had them the day before. She was a fast learner.

He secured Bear behind the wagon, then opened the flaps on the other side, revealing his goods.

When the first customer approached, Sarah squeezed herself into the same place as the day before, hidden from view. He almost wished she would challenge him with another offer to help. He enjoyed their banter.

But alas, he didn't want to jeopardize the relationships

he'd built with these folks, as they had only seen him alone all these years. Questions would arise. Questions he wasn't prepared to answer.

In truth, he had no idea what to do in this situation, and neither did she. He just knew they had to protect their reputations as much as possible.

Seven

After traveling a few days together I feel as if I know Miss Baker in a
completely new way. What Lord, do you intend by all this?

—From the journal of Alex Sinclair

As the last customer left, Sarah rose to her knees within the wagon while Alex lowered the flap. The silence in the air was a stark contrast to the lively conversation of the past hour.

Even though her leg hurt less today, she had to push through the pain as she helped stack the empty crates and baskets. It was important to her to be useful. To repay Alex.

Her stomach grumbled. Most of the baskets were empty. Was there anything to eat before they moved to the next stop? She didn't see any more soda crackers, which settled her stomach while they rode.

"Miss Baker?"

She put down the basket, moved to the edge of the opening, and stuck her head out. "Yes?"

"I've been calling ye a few times. Ye okay?" Alex handed her some jerky. "It's not much, but it will have to hold us until we can buy more. We need to head out if we're to arrive before dark."

"Sorry, I was concentrating." She bit into the hard, cold jerky. Anything in her stomach would be better than nothing.

He furrowed his brow. "What were ye so focused on?" He peeked inside. "Wow. Ye did all that. Thank ye, lass. Are ye ready?" He lifted a hand. "Let me help ye down."

Sarah studied Alex's extended hand for a moment before she placed hers in it. His calloused fingers caused a spark when they touched hers, and an unexpected flicker of heat traveled up her arm. Was it gratitude or something else? As she touched the ground, her leg wobbled, and he held her waist gently with his other hand. She swayed into his solid strength. Might be something else. She wobbled as she leaned away from him.

"Easy. How's the leg today?"

As much as she didn't want her injury to be a burden, she would use it to create some distance. "It's better. Let me walk a bit before we sit down."

He nodded and removed his hands. The warmth went with him.

She hobbled a few steps while her mind made sense of her emotions. When she glanced over her shoulder, she caught him staring at her foot with a frown on his face. "I'm good. See?" Now that the kinks were out, she stood straighter and focused all her attention on walking as normal as possible. It got easier as she went, so she kept going until she reached a set of bushes. Far enough away for some privacy. She peeked over again to make sure he wasn't still staring, but he was not there.

Relief flowed through her. Having his eyes on her affected her more than she wanted to admit.

Finishing her business, she headed back to the wagon, circling around to the front.

He was waiting on her side of the bench, leaning against the wood with his eyes closed. There was a peacefulness on his face, and his lips moved without any sound.

"Everything okay?" she asked.

He jumped. Opened his eyes. "Aye. Just thanking the Lord for what we've been given. And asking for his mercy as we move on."

"I didn't mean to interrupt." Her ears burned at interrupting his private moment.

"Nae, lass. It's no bother." His mouth opened and closed before he spoke again. "I hate to ask this of you, but we'll have to push harder to get to Vacaville by nightfall. I'll do my best to not cause you distress. If necessary, inform me of your need to stop, and I will. Deal?" He reached out a hand to help her into the wagon, even though she'd already proved she could do it herself.

The few bites of jerky landed with a thud in her stomach. She was determined to *not* cause him any delay.

"Deal." For the second time within the past hour, she placed her hand in his as he lifted her into the seat. The warmth from earlier returned, but she pushed it aside. There was no room for those thoughts.

He waited by her side while she adjusted her skirts, and still didn't move. "Lass, I see it in your face. Don't be making sacrifices on my account now."

She glanced at him. How did he know?

"I see the wheels churning in that mind of yours. Determination. Ye have it in spades. And I appreciate that. But if ye need to stop, ye need to stop. It won't upset me."

It was one thing to have to deal with a sour stomach, but another to talk about it over and over again. She faced forward and raised her chin. "I won't need to stop." She gripped the seat. "We should go."

He chuckled and tapped on the wood. "Aye, lass."

Within moments, he pulled himself onto his side of the bench and grabbed the reins. "Ready?"

She didn't want to look at him, but his eagerness to do right by her had her swiveling her head his way. A small smile escaped as she answered. "Ready."

In some ways, he treated her like a traveling companion, not a guest. As if he had accepted her presence with him on this journey. But she could be reading that wrong. He was a gentleman and had a caring nature. Since he mentioned having sisters, perhaps this was his typical behavior toward them.

One thing was certain. She did not want to complain. Already she had made him miss a stop and slowed him down. She was an extra mouth to feed, and her presence could affect his reputation. In all ways, she was a burden. Something she had felt since her parents died. The Taylors had to take her in. Been responsible for her. Luke had to marry her for her to stay under the same roof. Would she be a burden to others her whole life?

Alex said it wouldn't be an inconvenience to stop, but why did she feel like her presence was just that?

Once her leg healed fully, she would move on. It was the least she could do. So why did her heart ache at the thought of leaving?

* * *

Alex gave all his attention to holding the reins and facing forward, even though he wanted to squirm under the weight of Sarah's gaze on him. He didn't want her to think she was a burden. She wasn't. At least not anymore. Having her along was different now, but he didn't want to reflect on why. He'd say it was because he knew her story and understood her better.

And he cared.

Which always landed him in a heap of trouble. He just hoped he'd be on time for the prayer meeting he was supposed to speak at. He'd been looking forward to that stop for a while now, and he didn't want to miss. He wasn't sure what to do with Sarah once he arrived. Church was not a place where a single man and woman should be showing up together.

At least the wagon was empty, and they could travel faster. He'd make fewer stops for selling and focus on purchasing more supplies. They needed to save the time.

Twenty minutes later, Alex had formed some sort of plan. He considered the stops they would pass and which of the smaller towns were the best to stay overnight without anyone bothering them. Keeping Sarah safe was imperative. Communities where no one would recognize him and question why he had a lass with him.

He realized there'd been no words spoken, and he glanced over to make sure Sarah was awake.

She held her body stiff and gripped the seat hard enough her knuckles were white. She looked at him. "What?"

He smiled. "You mean, whit?"

Her face relaxed, and she smiled before facing forward again, her grip not so tight as before. He liked when his words added color to her face. And eased her mind from the motion. They had miles to go.

The wagon dipped into the hollow of a small hill, turning into a sharp bend and then another. Alex pulled the reins to slow them down, then leaned to the right, colliding with Sarah.

"Oof." She pushed at his arm.

"Sorry, lass." As much as he wanted to, he didn't dare lose focus or let go with one hand.

She wiggled to the far side of the bench, but the wagon swayed again and sent her right back into him. Her body pressed against his, and he fought to ignore the sensations the connection caused.

"Hold on. We're almost through this section. Must've had a lot of rain in the area." He led Bear far to the side to avoid the deeper ruts left by the stagecoaches. Sarah's leg pressed against his, and as much as he wanted to place a respectable space between them, he'd have to wait until they reached the straight part. *Lord, keep us safe.*

He hoped the swaying wasn't too unpleasant for her. Wagon seats weren't designed for comfort and space. They were functional for sitting up high and guiding the horses.

A whimper came from his companion, and he knew without looking that she'd hit a rough patch too. He scanned the surrounding area, searching for a safe place to pull over. The road curved ahead amongst trees and thick foliage. Great for her privacy, not so great for parking a peddler cart off the road. Any oncoming stagecoach or buggy would run into them if he stopped.

Should he acknowledge she wasn't feeling well? Would that make it worse or better? His mind blanked from finding a safe topic to distract her. He clenched his fingers around the reins as she shifted beside him. Heard her whimper and groan. *Lord, let her stomach hold steady. Help me find a smooth stretch of road soon.*

"I ... I ..."

"Hang on, Sarah. We're almost to where I can pull over. I know it's difficult. You're doing great." As much as he wanted to peek over, he couldn't. His eyes needed to stay on the road.

The last bend straightened out to a wider area, and Alex directed Bear to the side. "Whoa." Once the wagon stopped, he sat unmoving, catching his breath. Slowly, he turned to face Sarah. But she wasn't there. She was already out of the wagon and running to the copse of trees they had passed.

He wished he could do something to help her. Anything. But motion sickness was different for each person. He had a friend who struggled with it, unless he rode his own horse, which he ended up doing every time he traveled.

Did Sarah ride? As soon as he considered the question, he realized she wouldn't be able to with her injured leg or the clothes she wore. Did he even have the funds to buy a horse? A safe and calm one? Would that even be appropriate?

What had he gotten himself into when he agreed she could come along?

Movement from the side grabbed his attention as she pulled herself back onto the bench. She didn't say a word. Just fluffed out her skirts and settled onto the hard wood. Her pale face looked haggard and her eyes a bit dull, but the fact she was able to get on and off on her own showed a quiet strength.

"Need more time?"

"Nae." She smirked at him.

He laughed. As much as she slowed him down, *and* she shouldn't even be out in the wilderness with him, he enjoyed her company. For now, they didn't have much choice, so he would leave things in God's hands and be thankful they were both healthy and whole.

Now that Sarah had her stop, they could continue their journey. The journey that had become much more than stopping and selling goods. He didn't have the words for what it was, but his heart beat accelerated with the prospect of finding out.

Eight

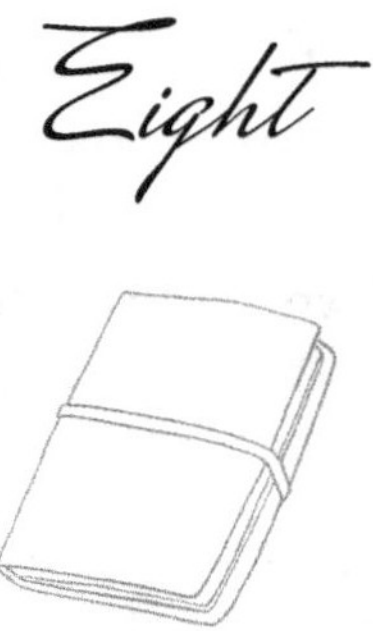

The need to protect Miss Baker's reputation weighs heavily on my shoulders. But I'm not able to control everything. Protect her, too, Lord.

—From the journal of Alex Sinclair

Over the next four hours Sarah gritted her teeth more than once as her body attempted to rebel against the rocking of the wagon. Determined to not make Alex stop more than necessary, she adjusted her body to reduce the impact. Shifting into various positions every ten minutes made a difference.

But then she created a new problem every time she bumped her companion's arm.

He'd smile and nod at her, understanding full well what she was doing.

She could admire the appreciation in his eyes all day. There was joy there too. Deep inside. When he smiled, the crinkled skin around his eyes would lift, as if they were smiling too.

They didn't say much since it was difficult to hear over the creaking wood, Bear's hooves hitting the ground, and the reins clanging. But Alex would point at things, yell a few words about the area they passed, or tell a story about a previous visit.

"We're close to where we'll restock. There's a spot I've camped at before that would be a good place for us, aye?" He glanced her way.

She nodded, holding the position that worked for her at that moment. The fact he said we and us in his sentence warmed her insides. Helped her not feel so alone. And something else Sarah didn't want to examine too close. Did he say it on purpose? Or did it just come out?

In the distance rooftops appeared, all lined up next to each other. They hadn't passed much in the way of communities, so this must be a larger town. Which meant more people.

Excitement coursed through her. There'd be streets and shops, possibly a dry goods store with pre-made dresses. She frowned. Not without funds. And she refused to impose on Alex any more than she had to. The dress would have to wait.

Alex slowed Bear to a stop. Glanced around. Nodded. "We'll stay here for the night."

Dust particles floated in the air as the mid-afternoon sunshine filtered through the trees from the west. There wasn't much to the spot he selected. Flat dry ground, remnants of a campfire left by someone else, and a creek flowing to the side.

She lowered herself to the ground, went to the back of the wagon, and pulled out a crate. Her leg, stiff after sitting all day, ached, yet she carried on.

Alex followed with the campfire box. After placing it near the pit, he stood and scratched the back of his head, tilting his hat forward. "I need to go to town and replenish my supply.

And you'll need to stay behind." His eyes wouldn't meet hers. "I won't be long."

She paused in pulling a piece of wood out of the tinder box. "What?"

He toed the box with his boot. "I need ye to stay here. It's too risky for ye to come with me."

Alone? That wasn't what she had expected. She forced a nod, but when she opened her mouth, her voice wavered. "You really think that's safer?"

He nodded. "Aye. I need to fully restock. Ye said ye know how to use a gun. I'm leaving ye my rifle and will help ye start the fire. No one will travel by at this time of the day."

"How can you be so sure?" Tears threatened as she grappled for control of her emotions.

"I just know." He stalked off, taking his hat and hitting his thigh with it before putting it on his head. It was obvious he didn't like this arrangement either.

She blinked a few times before placing the wood in the firepit.

He swiveled back to face her. "Look, lass, I don't like leaving ye alone, but yer strong enough to handle it, and it's only a wee while. If ye show up in town with me, yer reputation will be ruined. I don't think yer ready for that. I'm not ready for that. I'm in no position to offer for ye."

"You would offer for me?" Vague images of a life with Alex flashed in her mind, and she tried hard to ignore them.

He lifted his eyes toward the sky, the sun casting an orange-yellow glow on his face. "Nae, leave it to a lassie to focus only on a few of the words I spoke." His gaze found hers, and a strong glint appeared in his eyes. "Aye, I'm a man and consider myself a gentleman. But this is me livelihood, and I have no intention of marrying right now. I've no way to provide for a wife." He pointed at her.

Her cheeks reddened. "I never ... I wasn't asking ..."

His arms dropped to his sides and he sighed, the sound echoing in the quiet around them. "I know. But since our talk the other night, don't think the thought hadn't crossed my mind. More than once. I see what's going on inside yer heart." He paused and sighed again. "Yer a good person. I want what's best for ye."

She stood still, her mouth agape. Tears burned her eyes.

He stormed back toward her and opened his arms. "Come here."

Her forehead creased as she tried to make sense of the man before her. She approached him, and he reached out and gave her a brief side hug and a pat on the back. "You'll be fine."

Then he swung around and hustled to the front of the wagon, calling over his shoulder, "I'll be back as quickly as I can."

Sarah remained in the same place long after the dirt settled and she could no longer see the wagon or Alex. Her one lifeline to a new life had driven out of reach. She shivered, but not from the cool air that blew over her skin as the sun rested at the top of the next hill.

Would he come back for her? Or was she truly on her own?

Dropping her arms, she scanned the small area where she'd wait. Added a piece of wood to the fire. Listened for any out of place sound. Stacked a set of rocks to use as a table. Anything to keep busy and not dwell on the fact she was out in this wild land by herself. How could he just leave her?

After several minutes, she took the empty crate and headed for the nearest tree. Anything to lean on so she didn't feel so alone. Hunger long forgotten, she had finally settled against the trunk and dozed off when rattling wheels and clanking noises woke her. She scrambled to her feet, rifle in hand. She couldn't see anything in the dark.

"It's Alex, Sarah," a voice called out.

She relaxed and lowered the rifle, gratitude filling her heart at hearing his familiar brogue. The wagon drew near, but the shadows made it difficult to see clearly. Bear pulled and strained with the weight. Alex's journey into town must've been successful. She hoped he had fresh food in there. She was starving.

He pulled in but didn't say much as he unhitched Bear and led him to fresh grass. The routine similar to the other night, they worked in tandem to prepare a meal, although this time their dinner included fresh meat and biscuits Sarah made with the ingredients Alex had purchased.

Their plates emptied, he leaned against a fallen log and stared at the fire. "We need to make this food last as we pass through smaller towns. There won't be much for us between here and the next stop."

She nodded but didn't say anything. What was there to say? Even with his use of we, she was still a passenger tagging along, not knowing what was to come. She thought she'd enjoy the freedom, but the unknown grew tiresome. She craved the comfort of routine and the freedom to walk around town. She hadn't thought through the fact he couldn't acknowledge her in public, and she'd have to hide every time they encountered people. Not the future she wanted. A good reason she shouldn't form an attachment.

As it should be. But still. It was hard not to be drawn to this man who treated her with such respect and care.

She missed Michael, and what they shared, but she realized now it was a young girl's love. Of someone who paid attention to her when she was sad and alone. She could see that now. Michael would want her to be happy. To choose someone who would treat her well. He said as much as he laid on his deathbed, Sarah clinging to his hand and begging him not to leave her. She hadn't had time to understand her grief and put it into perspective.

Until now.

Being on her own helped her see things clearer than before. So why was the man before her all that she saw?

* * *

The next morning Sarah and Alex rose ahead of the sun, packed their bedrolls into the back of the wagon and left in the dark. Sarah knew Alex was trying to gain as much daylight for traveling in later. Yet with no idea where they were, and not being able to see, she had difficulty preparing for the sudden turns and jolts the road manifested.

"Our next major stop is the city of Fairfield. We could resupply there, if needed. Fairfield is the Solano County seat, so there are county buildings in town."

As much as she wanted to see a larger city and what county buildings looked like, she doubted Alex would take the risk. "I've never seen county buildings before."

"Aye. I'm sorry, lass. Maybe one day you'll be able to. I might travel around the city, rather than through it, so we don't bring attention to ourselves. Especially with you sitting upfront with me."

He was right, of course. But the missed opportunity still stung. Talking about all the places they passed was very different than seeing them.

The sun finally provided enough light for the landscape to be fully visible, but there wasn't much to see. The dry grass, green leaves on the trees, and dirt all looked the same as yesterday's scenery.

Whenever possible, Alex pulled over to find a water source so they could rest and replenish their canteens. She welcomed the breaks to settle her stomach, but the pace was slow, and her ability to gauge time and distance shrank with each stop.

The urge to ask how much farther grew, but she didn't want to disturb the comfortable silence. She imagined herself small and unobtrusive to keep some distance between them on the unyielding wooden bench. It was the toughest thing she'd ever done.

After another stop, Alex set a slow pace again, and the ruts in the road caused the wagon to sway. Sometimes a deeper hole jolted her spine hard against the seat. She had no choice but to hang on to Alex. A few times their thighs touched as they rocked, creating a different response in her stomach.

Did he feel it too? She didn't dare look at him, certain her cheeks were red enough to match her hair.

Alex pulled off the road and the wagon lurched, sending the crates rattling in the back. He yanked the reins, his muscles straining as Bear reared. Sarah's fingers clawed for a grip, but before she could steady herself, the whole thing tilted at an odd angle, causing her to fall into Alex's lap.

"Whoa. Easy boy," Alex called out.

Bear snorted and stomped his hooves in protest, then settled.

Silence engulfed them.

Sarah tried to push herself up, but gravity moved against her.

Two large hands grasped her upper arms and pulled her back. Concern etched Alex's brows. "Are ye okay?"

She nodded. A few bruises maybe, but nothing serious. "What happened?"

"We broke a wheel." He gritted his teeth. "We might be here a while." He shook his head and muttered while he tied the reins down.

Sarah scanned the area. There wasn't a person, wagon, or

town in sight. In fact, they hadn't seen anyone since earlier this morning.

Her heart pounded. What were they going to do?

Nine

Sometimes things don't go the way I want them to. No matter how much I prepare. Please forgive my frustration. My dependance on myself that I lean on when trying to fix things my way.

—From the journal of Alex Sinclair

Sarah's eyes grew wide with concern when Alex held her in his arms. He wished he could ease her fears, but fixing a wheel with a full load would take time. They were on a main road. Staying visible while they waited for assistance would not benefit either of them. She needed propriety. He could use some help. This broken wheel added an unwanted layer of complication they didn't need.

He jumped down from the seat and walked over to study the lilting side. Sure enough, a broken wheel. There was an extra one on the side of the wagon, but his tools were buried under all his goods. It was not midday yet, but perspiration ran down his back. They were going to swelter in the heat with no tree nearby to offer shade.

"Miss Baker, you might want to put a bonnet on. This will take a few hours." Maybe if he used her proper name, he could set some distance between them.

Out of the corner of his eye, he saw her flinch and recoil. She jumped from the bench seat without waiting for his help.

In this circumstance, he appreciated her independent streak. But his heart shriveled a bit at causing her pain. If she could stand up to him, he could swallow his pride and ask for a lady's help. "Aye, I can fix it. But we need to empty the wagon to reach me tools. Do ye mind helping?"

"I'll do whatever needs doing." She climbed into the wagon. Handed him each crate and basket without complaint. An hour later the wagon was emptied and all his goods were in piles on the ground.

He found his extra support tools and went to work on lifting the wagon. Once Alex had it in position, he removed his hat and crawled on the dried grass to get underneath. His back was in the dirt, his hands grimy from twisting parts on and off when he heard a rumbling. It grew louder. In the middle of the repair and unable to stop, he called out. "Sarah?"

He heard her footsteps before seeing her boots. "Yes?"

"What's that noise?" Somehow he knew but wanted her confirmation.

She squatted and their eyes met. "Wagons are coming this way. A whole group of them." Her brow furrowed. "Is this a good thing or bad thing?"

He grunted while trying to unscrew the last bolt. "Well, it could be both. Aye, I could use a little help fixing the wheel, if they stop and offer assistance. However ye being an unmarried lady alone with me would not be wise information to share with them. We must pretend we're married." He focused his gaze on her. "Agreed?"

At this point he would do anything to protect her. She

hadn't done anything wrong, but they didn't need the complication of their situation making things worse.

She froze. Her face paled as the ramifications sank in.

He could watch her mind work all day long.

Her gaze searched the ground before finding his again. She nodded. "I agree. Although I'm not quite sure how a young married couple is supposed to behave."

He returned to his repairs, smiling on the inside at her innocence. "We'll figure it out. For now, why don't ye stand watch and let me know when they're close?"

"Yes, dear."

Her playful reply caused an unexpected sensation in his belly.

He closed his eyes. Ever since he agreed for Miss Sarah Baker to join him, nothing had been predictable. His eyes startled open and his heart lurched as he realized he had no complaint. *Lord, is this your plan for me?*

There was no time to dawdle on his feelings. He refocused on the wheel.

Unfamiliar voices grew near, then one distinct voice rose above the rest. "Our wheel broke. My h-husband is fixing it, but he might need help."

Alex didn't like placing Sarah in this position. She hadn't notified him in time, and now he wasn't making the introduction. Although, as he listened to the conversation, the way she handled herself filled him with pride.

"Mighty obliged to offer assistance, ma'am. What's your husband's name?"

"Mr. Smith," she answered.

Alex winced, wishing she knew his true name. He hadn't desired to share that with anyone until now.

"But you may call him Alex."

He smiled even though no one could see him under the wagon.

Black boots appeared before the man with the deep, gruff voice said anything. "Smith, my name is Jones. May I offer help?"

Alex climbed out from under the wagon. "Hal-low, Jones. I could use another pair of strong hands to lift this wheel on and hold it in place while I twist the bearings."

Together they took off the broken wheel and attached the spare. He climbed back under the wagon, and as the weight lifted, Alex clicked the pieces together properly and rotated the center until it was secure. He wiped his hands on the ground, rubbing the grease off before pulling himself out and up. He reached out a hand. "Thanks for the lift."

"No problem. Are you headed west?"

"We are."

"I see you have a full wagon. Are you a peddler?"

"I am."

"We could use some replacement supplies. Would you be able to open shop today?"

Alex was exhausted and needed the wares for the next town, but he wasn't going to say that. The thought of setting his wagon up in this heat made his neck sweat. "I think we can do that. Can ye give us a bit to get everything set to rights?"

"Not a problem. I'll go notify the rest of the group that we plan to stay a while. Maybe since it's getting later, we'll set up camp here."

Alex froze.

How would he and Sarah keep up the charade of husband and wife if these folks stayed the night?

* * *

Sarah halted folding the coarse blanket she held in her hands and turned to look at Alex. Never did she think she'd hear him say those words. She tamped down the happy smile twitching in her lips. She had no intention of showing any eagerness. "Did you say something?" She finished folding and held the blanket close to her middle even though it prevented any breeze to cool her from the warm sun.

He paused and narrowed his eyes. "Aye, ye like me asking for yer help, don't ye?"

"Well, it *is* nice to be needed." She wouldn't add that she enjoyed his attention.

"Let me tell ye what it is first, lass, and then ye can decide." He smirked.

Didn't matter. She'd do anything for this gentleman who had shown nothing but kindness to her.

"The travelers would like us to open up shop so they can see what we have."

She scanned the piles stacked neatly by the wagon. Everything was in disarray. "Now?"

"Aye." He placed his hands on his hips and sighed. "I know. I'd like yer help getting it all back inside. How about ye climb in, and I'll hand ye things to put away."

There he went putting her needs before his. It would leave him out in the sun. "But I don't know where everything goes."

"I'll tell you." He waited for a response, but she didn't give one. "Think of it as an adventure."

She laughed at his use of her favorite word. This would give her something to do. Not to mention she'd get to handle everything he had to sell. "Put that way, okay. But you have to let me help sell too."

She watched the muscles on his face contort as he fought the need to let go of control. If they told this small group they were married, partners for life, then they had to show that she was a partner in his peddler business too. She didn't know whether she would do a good job or not, nor if she would like it, but she wanted to try. "I'll listen to your direction. Promise."

His stiff posture eased, hinting at his relenting. She was getting better at reading him.

"All right. Ye can help sell. But only because they think you're my wife."

A flutter twirled in her stomach. She hoped it wasn't the food she ate earlier.

It happened again as he placed his hands around her waist and lifted her into the back of the wagon. She brushed at her skirts till her stomach settled and then went to work. She didn't know what it meant, nor was there time to ponder.

He handed her a pile of dishes. "These go at the bottom to the left."

"Got it. Bottom left." She bent and placed them under the lower shelf.

Then he handed her a chest. "Careful, it's heavy. This goes next to the plates."

Her hands switched places with Alex's on the handles, but he didn't let go. Instead he placed them on top of hers, the size and warmth covering them completely. She looked up at his face and he smiled, appreciation sparkling in his eyes. She almost let go of the case, but his hands held hers. She tightened her grip and nodded for him to get something else. "You can let go. I've got it."

He let go slowly, watching her the entire time.

She spun around and hit her head on the wood. "Oof."

"Ye okay in there?"

Her face heated. She took a deep breath to steady her words. "Yes, just fine. I'll be ready for the next item in a moment."

She came back to the opening and Alex leaned inside. "Ye sure yer okay?" Concern etched his features.

Warmth radiated throughout her body. It had been a while since anyone showed concern for her in any way. And for something as small as hitting her head on a silly little piece of wood. Her stomach fluttered again, and she brushed her hands together and tried to act normal. "Never better. Whit will you hand me next?" She giggled at her mimic of his pronunciation of the word "what."

He raised his eyebrows but didn't speak.

Her heart longed to hear him say *my heart* in answer to her question, but that was wishful thinking. He had made his intentions clear and she knew without a doubt he would never hand her his heart. Even though her mind understood that truth, she would somehow have to convince her own heart of that fact.

* * *

ALEX HANDED Sarah a light basket full of linens. "These go across from the plates."

She nodded and went to set the wicker in the correct place. Her knees cracked as she bent into the small area, and the basket scraped across the wood boards.

His canteen lay on the grass too far to reach, so he swallowed the dust that settled in his mouth while he watched her before reaching for the next set of supplies. Sweat dripped into his eyes, and he lifted his hat and wiped his sleeve across his forehead, providing time to gather his thoughts. Having spent the past few days with the lady, he knew she expressed her thoughts and feelings easily. Her quietness created a sense of unease.

Something was bothering her. But there wasn't time to ask.

He lifted a solid wood crate and set it on the back of the wagon bed. "Place these in the front corner." He held on to the rope handles as her hands reached for them. The skin-on-skin contact sent vibrations up his arms.

Her gaze met his and she raised her eyebrows. Did she feel it too?

He grinned, hoping to instigate some sort of similar reaction.

It didn't. She shook her head, her green eyes lowered. When she pulled away, she focused on setting those goods in their resting place, the scrape of wood on wood louder than before.

Had he said something wrong?

The itch to sit with her, alone, talking about everything and anything competed with the sweltering heat, but they had company. And he had a job to do. Which included protecting her reputation. Avoiding repercussions when this group parted was imperative. She could come across any of these people again in her travels when she left him.

The thought of saying goodbye made him ill.

Yet he'd have to walk away. Someday.

For now, he had to organize his supplies to sell to these strangers and leave as soon as possible. There would be time to deal with whatever was bothering Sarah later.

They continued working with only his directions as conversation, until he picked up the last crate. "This holds material for a wedding or a bride's trousseau." He tossed the words out, and they landed like bricks on either side of them.

She grabbed at the crate, careful to not touch his hands. Her gaze didn't meet his either.

Before she could pull away, he gripped her wrist. "Something is bothering ye. Whit is it?"

She bit her lip and his stomach dipped. Yet she still didn't make eye contact. "I'm fine. Just a little nervous about playing the role of your wife, that's all."

The word wife caused a scene in his mind to appear. One where she became exactly that. He swallowed. "Aye." Not knowing what else to say, he dropped her arm and helped her settle the box in its place. The situation was awkward and would get more so as the night progressed. Maybe these were nerves he felt too.

But in his gut, he knew it was more.

There was no way to avoid the next few hours, though. Was it wrong he looked forward to this time of pretend?

He scratched the back of his neck as he watched her place the last of the goods in its spot and brush her hands together. "Anything else?"

He glanced around before returning his gaze on her again. "That's all. Everything is clean and well-organized." Much faster than when he did it himself. Why had he not allowed her to help sooner?

She reached for a sack and placed it in a new home, her movements purposeful. She'd organized his wagon better than he ever could. His chest tightened. She had taken to this life so easily. Too much so. And for a dangerous second, he imagined a world where this wasn't pretend.

He dropped his arms and took a step back. "Let's open shop, then. Why don't ye stay here, and I'll let the others know." He hurried toward the group of wagons. His heart accelerated as his mind tried to block out the vision.

Why had those images intruded his mind? She was not supposed to be here. With him. Near him.

Helping him. At least, that's what he kept repeating to remind himself. But other thoughts crept in as well. Like how easy she was to talk with. How he could be himself when he was around her. How delightful she was to look at and tease.

He enjoyed watching her face show a million expressions while she found the words to throw back at him. How she never complained. Even willing to ride for miles in a wagon knowing it caused her belly to turn.

She deserved happiness. She deserved an adventure. The loss she experienced as a child haunted her, and he wanted to replace those memories with new ones.

Yet she needed someone who could commit. And he couldn't. If he was anyone but Alexander Sinclair, he would be free to marry her. But he wasn't.

He shook off those thoughts. Today was about peddling goods—together. A first step toward providing the adventure she sought. And giving her skills she could use in her future.

It would have to be enough.

Ten

Sarah stood inside the wagon, a basket in her grip as Alex crossed the field and approached the newcomers. Had he left her in charge of the supplies? Her heart accelerated, and she winced from the fibers poking into her palm.

As Alex moved from the first group to the next, a woman turned and headed her way.

Her first customer.

She quickly set down the container and brushed her hands on her skirt. Her stomach rolled as she replayed what Alex had said the day before about how to talk with the customer. He made this look so easy.

The older woman approached the open side of the wagon.

"May I help you find something?"

The woman had a tow-headed boy in her arms and an older daughter clinging to her skirt. The boy lifted his head, and when Sarah smiled at him, buried his face in the crook of his mother's neck.

"Do you have any play things?" the woman asked. Her face was drawn, and her clothes wrinkled. "A ball, hoop, anything?"

Sarah understood immediately. "I might have just the thing. Let me look."

She had seen a wooden toy wagon in one of the crates earlier. After lifting a few things, she found it. Leaning out the window she spoke to the boy. "Is this to your liking?"

As he clung to his ma, he lifted his eyes warily.

Sarah held the toy out with her left hand and with her right, spun the wheels. "All four wheels move. And it's small enough to carry around. You can even tow it behind you as if you're the horse or ox."

The boy stared at the plaything long enough to let Sarah know he wanted it. Reaching for it would be a different story.

The mother glanced at her daughter standing next to her. "Tell the nice lady what you would like as well."

The girl shook her head. "Ma, we don't have any funds to buy something so frivolous."

"Now hush. This is something your father would've wanted had he survived our trek west. The least I can do is honor what he would want for his daughter."

Sarah's heart hurt for the young girl who'd lost her father. Close to Sarah's age in fact, when she lost her own pa. She reached into the linens and pulled out a lace neckerchief. Something small and special. She placed it on the ledge of the wagon. "I lost my father when I was fourteen. It hurt something fierce. Still does. But he gave me something before I lost him, and I always carry it with me. It's a gift to communicate you're growing up and you're loved. If you're purchasing with his funds, in my mind, this would be a gift from him."

The girl's cheeks colored as a slow smile spread across her face. She didn't reach for the fabric but glanced to her mother for approval.

Her mother's eyes filled with tears. Her voice wobbled. "How much?"

Sarah looked at the toy wagon and the neckerchief and wanted so badly to give both items to them. A throat cleared and Alex approached from the side. Her tears welled behind her eyelids.

"Both of them together would be thirty cents," he answered.

The relief on the woman's face was immediate. Alex ruffled the young boy's hair, took the wagon from Sarah's hands, and held it out to the boy. He finally let go of his mother's neck and latched on to the toy. The young'un wiggled and asked his mother to set him down and ran toward his wagon. The girl stepped forward and handled the neckerchief with so much care, she didn't even put a crease in it. The woman handed Alex the coins.

He put his hands behind his back. "No, ma'am. She's the one who made the sale. You can hand her the coins. Besides, the money box is inside." The woman nodded her thanks and handed Sarah the thirty cents.

Sarah closed her fingers around the coins, the metal warm on her skin. Giddy from her first sale, her heart soared. The simple act of making two children and their mother happy was unlike anything she'd experienced. Her emotions from the transaction were indescribable.

"Thank you both for helping make a difficult situation better." The mother smiled at them before she turned and headed back the way she came with the girl holding her gift with both hands as she talked to her mother.

The spring in their steps caused Sarah's heart to skip. She glanced at Alex through the canvas flap. "What just happened?"

* * *

Sarah's question echoed in Alex's head as he waited until the mother and her children were far enough away. She didn't utter a word but tilted her head in that way she did, as if trying to piece together a puzzle. A smart woman, she understood he'd not made a profit on the sale.

He raised his brow, daring her to question him further.

Instead, her lips lifted into a beautiful smile. A genuine one, where her tongue peeked through her teeth. He'd noticed this habit of hers the first day. Something she was unaware of and so subtle most would miss it. But not Alex. It was not a forced smile, but one reflecting true joy in the moment.

Alex was taught from a young age to pay attention. To his studies, his servants, and his tenants. What he could gather through observation would be more than answers from demanded questions. It was how he caught someone with impeccable manners hiding a closed fist or a forced smile that didn't quite reach the eyes. These things revealed more than words ever could.

Sarah's eyes shone with light and curiosity. She didn't hold back. Had unlimited amounts of passion and energy. It was refreshing and at the same time dangerous. For him. Every instinct told him to step back and create distance. Yet her light drew him in.

"You sell your goods below cost on a regular basis, don't you?" Her gaze held his.

"Aye." He tried not to fidget under her scrutiny.

"Now I understand why." She glanced toward the other wagons. "You want to help them, don't you? I felt it. Just now. The desire to hand over the items was so strong. But a handout was not what they needed, even though they do need help. Is that what you feel?"

"Aye." What did she want him to say?

"Is that why you didn't want me to help? Although, while sitting inside the wagon, I thought that was what you were doing."

He shrugged. "Partially. The reasons I mentioned the first day still stand. But to answer yer question, every day I see people struggle. I have regulars I check on. Women who hold down the homestead while their men are off working. Or husbands who never return. I pray for them too. When I'm selling to them and after. They stay in my mind, sometimes for months after."

"I don't think I will ever forget that mother and her two children."

He grinned and stepped closer. "You won't. They burrow themselves here." He placed his hand on his heart.

"You like this." She moved her arm in a circle. "It motivates you."

She was correct. He liked what he did. Helping these families, providing support and material goods to them. Offering encouragement and a prayer. It filled him. But he couldn't do it forever.

She fidgeted. "I think I need to come out now."

He walked to the back of the wagon and offered his hand to Sarah as she climbed down.

She faced him. "How did I do?"

He didn't release her hand. "Ye did great, lass. The toy wagon was the perfect item for the boy."

"And the girl?" Her eyes searched his.

"You could relate to her, couldn't you?"

Tears pooled in her eyes as she nodded. No words passed her lips, but he understood. He meant only to squeeze her hand, but somehow, she was in his arms, her warmth settling against him like she belonged there. She clung to him and a sob wrenched free.

"There, there, lass. It's okay." He'd had plenty of experience with his sisters when they needed to cry.

She pulled back and hiccupped. "You're something, you know that?"

He frowned. "I dinnae understand."

She swatted at his arm. "Not in a bad way. A good way. You understand me like no one else. You listen. You hug me when I need a hug. I've only known you a few days, and already you know me. No one has ever understood or paid attention."

"Not even yer brother?"

She bit her lip and studied the grass in the distance. "I don't know. I realize I'm not being very fair. He's been gone for so long, maybe I'm not remembering correctly."

"Maybe. Although yer feelings are real. Ye can't make them go away. At some point ye have to deal with them."

She studied him and her eyes narrowed. "What feelings have *you* dealt with while on this wild adventure of yours?"

He kept his composure open so she wouldn't see his reaction. It was one thing to read her, quite another for her to read him. Although if he was honest, she already had. Alex had finally met his match. Someone who was strong enough to not take his word at face value. Never in his twenty-five years had he encountered anyone like her.

She crossed her arms, waiting for an answer.

He needed to give one. Not the canned answer he gave

others, because she would see through that. He wrestled with the question. What had he dealt with while out on his own?

He had learned he could stand on his own two feet. The fear of standing up for himself and others was gone. The expectations of his family remained, but he didn't want to go home to them or his betrothed. He knew without a doubt he wanted to stay in California.

But with freedom came costs, and Alex wasn't quite ready to cut ties with his family. He needed more time away and more time with this beautiful creature standing in front of him. Why, he didn't know. "Ye ask what feelings have I dealt with?"

"Yes." A puff of dirt raised from the ground as she tapped her foot.

"Och. I'm tired of running."

Eleven

My heart is guarded. For good reason. How can I trust to lower the wall? When will I know it's safe?

—From the journal of Alex Sinclair

Running? Alex was running from something? Sarah rubbed her forehead. "I don't understand."

Footsteps approached, and they both turned as a man wearing a straw hat, a tan long sleeve shirt, and brown trousers came around the corner of the wagon.

"We wanted to invite you to join our group for dinner. We've planned a campfire program for the kids. They are restless. We've been on the trail a long time."

"Where are you headed?" Were they on the same trail?

The man scratched his neck. "Well, miss, our hope is to make it to the Napa Valley. Find work in them new wineries forming there."

Sarah had never heard of a winery. "Was that your original plan?"

"No, ma'am. We knew we wanted to make it to California. But Sacramento was too busy and most of the land already claimed in the area. When we heard of the wineries we moved on. We've all suffered losses. Want to land somewhere with a place we can call our own."

"Aye, you're on the right trail." Alex shook the man's hand. "Alex Smith."

"Morgan Clark." He studied Alex. "You've been there before?"

"Aye. Beautiful land." Alex's voice held a hint of awe.

"We'll have to talk more then. Would be helpful to have some idea of what to expect and possibly where to go. I hear it's a long valley."

"Bonnie it is. Several small towns with lots of land in between. The wineries are farther north of the main town of Napa."

"Much obliged. I need to get back and help with chores. See you at supper? No need to bring anything but your own tins."

Alex shook Mr. Clark's hand again.

Sarah waved, while her mind swirled in multiple directions. What would it have been like for her family to travel like this. The little boy and teenage girl she'd met earlier came to mind. Would she have lost her parents sooner or still have them? Would her brother have gone off to learn preaching? Would she be here right now, in the middle of nowhere, with a handsome man, pretending to be his wife?

As much as she had dreams, situations and events changed them. And would continue to do so throughout her life. She couldn't foresee when or where they would occur any more than she could guess when a wagon wheel would break. It was clearer now that how she reacted to these circumstances and what she made of them mattered.

Alex placed his hand at the small of her back and pressed

her forward to follow the man around the wagon. They stopped and watched him walk to the circle of wagons, but Alex didn't remove his hand. The pressure caused more tingles in her stomach, and she shivered.

"Are ye cold?"

She shook her head and faced him. "No, just nervous. We don't know these people, yet we're dining with them as well as sleeping near them. All while pretending to be husband and wife. Are you comfortable with this?"

"Aye and nae, lass. This is the life of a nomad. The part where we meet people along the way, interject ourselves in each other's lives. Learn something. Give something in return." He rubbed his neck. "The part where we pretend to be married? That's new. We need to ask for the Good Lord's guidance and protection there."

"Do you often join up with others?"

"Aye. Sometimes it's nice to have the company. Other times, I count the minutes till we part. Depends on their habits and their ways." There was a far off look in his eyes.

She waited. Absorbed what he said. Cleared her throat. "I hope you don't count down the minutes today."

His eyes found hers, and he furrowed his brows. "To leave this group?"

Sarah clasped her hands. "Well, sort of. I guess so we don't have to pretend. But I ..." She stared at the rock near her toe. Kicked it with her boot. "What I meant was for me to leave. I've been with you awhile. Changed your plans. Your route." She whispered the last few words.

He placed his hands on her shoulders. "Sarah, lass. Look at me."

She raised her head.

"Aye, having ye here on this journey is different. But I'm not lying when I say I've enjoyed yer company. It will be hard when we part ways." He held up a hand. "I don't know when that will be or where. I'm not going to leave ye somewhere unless ye want to be left. Even then, I would ensure your safety first."

She let out the breath she held. "I don't want to be a burden. But I don't know where I would go. I realize that now. The world is quite big out here." She gazed into the distance.

He lifted his hand and placed it under her chin, moving her head till her eyes caught his. "Nae. Ye are *not* a burden. Never have been. So get that out of yer head, lass. You're quite the opposite, in fact."

The intensity in his gaze brought back the fluttering in her stomach. "Oh! How so?"

"Well, I learned today ye see people as I see them. Ye cared more about them than the sale."

She swallowed, the lump in her throat fighting to go down.

He kept his eyes on hers, but they dipped to her lips and back up.

She stopped breathing.

And then the moment was gone.

His eyes no longer held tenderness, but something more like regret. He dropped his hand. "Let's grab our tins and head over to their camp for some grub."

ALEX ALMOST DID SOMETHING SELFISH. He'd never been reckless. He was a man who made plans, set goals, and followed through. But with Sarah, he was on the edge of something he couldn't control. The pull to kiss her caused him to forget himself. Who he was. What was expected of him. But aye, he wanted to kiss her. He was drawn to her like no other. She fascinated him. Made him laugh. Caused him to forget.

From the side of the wagon, he reached for the extra canvas at the top and lowered it in place, securing the lines tight. His motions wooden, he pushed himself to complete his task.

Sarah climbed into the wagon from the back and moved around inside. Gone was the bantering. The comments they each made while they worked. It was as if she was holding her breath, trying not to make a sound.

"Sarah, can ye hand me my guitar when you're finished?"

"Sure." She met him at the back of the wagon and handed him the guitar before he helped her down.

He pushed the panels closed and fastened the latches. Within moments, the wagon was locked up tight. It was time to pretend with his wife. "How's the leg?"

She glanced at her lower half. "It's better. I've been moving around all day, not thinking about it. It's tender, but I don't think I'm limping as much, do you?"

He shook his head. "Nae. I can only tell when you make a face."

Her gaze met his. "I don't hide my emotions well, do I?"

"Nae." He shook his head.

She laughed. "Will always pointed that out."

"It's not a bad thing. It keeps ye honest."

"True. But sometimes my feelings appear before I even know what they are. I don't want someone to understand them before I do. Nor read into them if I've already changed what they are."

He laughed. "Lass, there's not a wiser statement as that. Ready to go?"

"Ready as I'll ever be, husband." She turned her cheeky grin his direction.

His pulse raced, and he got tongue-tied. He had to get his act together. Or he would be the one showing feelings he didn't want seen. He placed his hand on her lower back as they walked to the other camp.

The wagon leader, Jones, raised his hand. "Welcome. So glad you could join us."

Alex leaned over and shook the man's hand, never losing touch with Sarah. "We appreciate the invitation. We don't get to visit with many people when on the road."

"I'm sure being a young married couple you don't mind the space."

Sarah stiffened at the reference of them being married.

He chuckled, moved his hand to her side, and pulled her closer. "Well, we don't complain, right lass?" He kissed her temple.

"When traveling with a group such as ours, there isn't much privacy for anyone." Jones looked over the camp.

Alex was sure he knew everyone's business.

Sarah's eyes grew wide.

He leaned into her and whispered in her ear. "Don't be embarrassed. He's not meaning anything by it, lass." He faced their host and changed the topic. "I brought my guitar. Thought I could play for ye all."

Several "all rights" and "yeses" filtered through the camp.

"That would be wonderful." Jones motioned to a bench. "We saved you some seats. Please, sit."

Alex helped Sarah sit on the log being used as a bench, then took the tins to the fire and received their food before returning to her. He closed his eyes. *Bless this food, Lord.* Then dug in.

The clanking of tins, murmurs of thanks, and appreciation for the food filled the camp. When everything was cleared away, Alex positioned his guitar. He strummed a few chords and then played a favorite of his. The upbeat tune always livened up a gathering.

Sure enough, several in the group clapped along. The

youngsters jumped up and down, holding hands as they danced in a circle. The girl Sarah sold the handkerchief to earlier came running over and grabbed Sarah's hand, pulling her into the fray.

Sarah laughed, not even looking back his way.

Alex strummed while he watched her join the children, her hair flowing down her back and her laughter filling the air. She was so full of life. He loved how she participated in whatever situation was thrown her way. And he couldn't take his eyes off her. The music, the crisp air, and the stars sparkling in the night as laughter filled their camp made tonight one of those moments Alex lived for. He would savor this memory for many years.

He'd put his head down and focused on the placement of his fingers, when someone tugged on his arm. So lost in the music, the touch startled him. He stopped and glanced up.

"Come dance with us." Sarah stood in front of him, beaming from ear to ear.

He frowned. "I'm playing."

"So are they." She pointed to a group of men who had joined in with a violin, another guitar, and a bongo drum.

"Come on. Take a break. It will be fun."

He set his guitar against the log, stood, and clasped her offered hand. Together they joined the group around the campfire. As they moved in a circle, they twisted and laughed. The joining of their hands sent warmth through him as they sang and danced to the rhythm.

Sarah glanced at him, and their eyes formed a connection that traveled all the way to his heart. Whatever it was, he didn't want it to end.

Soon the music stopped. Everyone clapped. Laughter bubbled up along with joy. He hadn't been that exuberant in a long while, and energy coursed through him.

Families with young children stood and called out goodnight. A signal for Sarah and him to leave as well. He picked up his guitar. Then they thanked their hosts and strolled back to their wagon with their hands still clasped together. What a night. Why did it have to go by so fast? "Did ye have fun?"

She grinned at him with her special smile, her tongue pushed up against her teeth. "I did."

He didn't know what else to say but didn't want the moment to end. "I'm glad."

"Did you have fun?"

He squeezed her hand. "Aye."

"We're having quite the conversation, aren't we?" She giggled.

He cleared his throat. "I think we're avoiding what comes next."

She raised their clasped hands. "What *is* next?"

He swallowed. "Well, lass. It looks like tonight we need to sleep under the wagon." He paused. "To keep up appearances." Alex faced her. "Sarah. Please trust me. I dinnae want you to feel uncomfortable." He let go of her hand.

"I know. I do trust you." Her lips lifted into a small smile.

"It's late, and it's been a long day. Let's get some sleep. We have an early morning tomorrow. Another day of travel."

She groaned. "Don't remind me."

He spread his arms wide, his guitar banging against his leg. "You wanted to come on this grand adventure."

A light shone in her eyes. "Aye. I'm so glad I did too. It has been an adventure. One I'm not ready to end yet."

He studied her. "Me, too, lass. Me too."

Her smile dimmed and she headed for the back of the wagon.

He followed. The magical moment over.

They grabbed their bedrolls and placed them under the wagon with a large heap of grass between them.

He laid on his side and rolled over to face the outside world.

"What are you doing?" she murmured.

"Giving ye your privacy. And keeping an eye out. I don't want my back against the open air."

"Oh," she whispered. "Will that look odd?"

Her innocence was endearing. He planned to keep it that way. "Not at all. I'm making it easier to spot trouble if it comes."

He glanced over his shoulder. They were close enough he could see her face in the dark. He winked.

She blinked back at him. Closed her eyes. "Goodnight."

Was that relief or disappointment in her eyes? Or were those his own emotions he struggled with? One thing was for sure. He could get used to more magical moments such as tonight with the red-headed, green-eyed beauty. If only he was free to do so.

"Goodnight lass." He rolled back over and faced the outside world.

Twelve

Thank you for your protection, Lord. I pray the rest of the journey is without incident.

—From the journal of Alex Sinclair

Morning light bounced off the ground next to Sarah as she awoke. She rolled over and found Alex already up, his bedroll gone. The events of the night before filtered through her mind as she rolled out from under the wagon, careful to not sit up too soon and bang her head.

She'd slept well. Maybe because she was more protected under the wagon. Not only from the elements, but also with Alex on guard nearby.

He was cooking breakfast over a small fire. "Coffee?"

Oh, she could kiss this man. "Thank you." She brushed off the dirt and grass from her hair and clothes and hurried over to accept the cup he held out for her. Her eyes closed as the first sip slid down her throat.

He chuckled.

They ate in silence, then cleaned everything and stored it safely in the wagon.

She climbed onto the wagon seat.

Alex frowned. "You could've waited for me, lass." He shook his head and finished harnessing Bear.

Sarah hadn't meant to injure his pride. She'd always managed without assistance. To not be a trial. Do what she could herself. But that didn't seem what he wanted her to do.

He pulled himself onto his side of the seat. "We still need to act like we're married, dear. Just until we are far enough away. What would they think if I don't help my lovely wife?"

That was the reason then. Sarah bit her lip. He thought she was lovely?

He shook his head and laughed. "I can see those wheels churning in that head of yers. Don't be too quick to read into my words, lass. Now wave goodbye to our hosts. We might see them again on this journey."

Sarah shifted toward the wagon train. Sure enough, many had stopped what they were doing and waved as they traveled by.

"Bye. Thanks for the festive night." She kept her hand raised until she had to face forward again to keep her stomach in one place.

The mother and two kids she'd helped yesterday came to mind, and she decided to pray for them and for their safe journey. She couldn't bow her head without feeling queasy, so she closed her eyes.

Tears rolled down her cheeks as her heart stirred anew. She had sat through dozens of church meetings back home, bowed her head at mealtimes without a second thought. But when Michael died, the prayers stopped, along with a connection to her heavenly father. She told herself it was grief, but now she saw it for what it was. Distance. A wall she had built between herself and God.

A wave of guilt overcame her. So mixed up in her own selfish thoughts about her pain, her freedom, and the need to escape a situation caused by no one in particular, she never grasped onto the one thing she missed most. But now that she had all the things she thought she needed, a hollowness remained inside. One only God could fill. The realization shook loose the cobwebs inside, much like the jostling from the ruts in the road caused the plates to rattle inside the crates. The shifting put things in order somehow.

"Lass? You okay?" Alex reached over and placed his hand on hers.

She opened her eyes. "Yes, I'm fine."

"Yer eyes were closed. Am I seeing tears? Are ye sad to say goodbye to our new friends?" Alex glanced at the road and back at her. "Not that I'm paying close attention or anything."

Her body warmed at his consideration. Most didn't notice when she became introspective. Actually she hadn't had time to be introspective. She tucked that realization away to examine later to focus on something he didn't say. He noticed things about her. Even the tiniest things. No man she had known had ever paid her the attention Alex had. And he wasn't even trying to court her.

No wonder she could fall for him. Even Michael, the one she pledged to marry, didn't ask when her thoughts turned deep and heavy. He just teased her until she forgot whatever plagued her. But was that what she had wanted? Someone who never saw beyond what they wanted her to be? What about her brother, Will? Would he see beyond her outer shell and the struggles within? Especially now that he was a preacher?

More guilt overcame her. Her brother would be worried.

"I'm thinking about my brother. I probably should write him and let him know I'm okay."

He nodded. "Ready to let someone know where ye are?"

"Something like that."

She needed God to know where she was too. Unlike requiring paper and pen to write a letter to Will, she could talk to God here and now. *I'm here, God. Ready to receive you. Not sure all I'm supposed to say. Maybe I'm sorry? Forgive me? I wanted to let you know I'm ready to open my heart again. I should've never closed it off. I know that now. For you're always with me. Help me see that clearer as we travel through this beautiful land you've created.*

She opened her eyes and glanced at Alex.

He studied her but didn't say anything. There was a shiny glint in his eyes. His gaze held a moment longer, then he winked before steering Bear around the next bend.

Sarah held onto the bench seat, expecting a wave of nausea to flood her system. But it never came. Instead a peace filled her. One she hadn't felt before. And for some reason, she didn't think it was because of the man sitting beside her.

* * *

ALEX WATCHED Sarah out of the corner of his eye. Something had changed. He hoped it wasn't due to the closeness they shared when holding hands last night or the awkwardness of pretending to be married. His protective nature wanted to jump in and dig for answers, but he observed her instead.

After another mile of peaceful companionship, he figured it out. There was a stillness about her. As if she had come to terms with something. His thoughts traveled in a circle till they landed on the only answer that made sense.

He hadn't been sure what God's plan was in bringing Sarah and him together. In the beginning, he was concerned about protecting her. And as much as it risked both their reputations, he hadn't minded her company. But now? The threads connecting them grew stronger than anything he'd experienced. Sure, he enjoyed good conversation and listening to other's stories. Sarah had a lot to say. And he'd listened.

He smiled. Glanced her way. The sight caused his heart to thump harder.

But there was much more to their relationship. It wasn't one-sided. Sarah listened to him too. And cared. He'd never had anyone take the time to get to know him. Most people focused on their own problems and didn't care to ask questions. He felt heard and understood by Sarah. That explained in part why he hadn't met anyone like her.

He glanced at her again. A warmth spread throughout his body. His mouth grew dry.

She sat with her hands in her lap, the wind blowing her red hair loose. Her skin color no longer looked green, just her eyes, and they shined with appreciation as she enjoyed the beauty around them.

She must've felt his gaze. "What?" Her eyes darted anywhere but toward him.

"I didn't mean to make you nervous, lass. You're riding more at ease today."

"I am." She grinned. "Mighty thankful for that too. Praise God."

"Praise him indeed." He loved hearing her talk about the Lord. "How about at the next rest we both write some letters? I'm overdue to send one to my family. I like to send regular updates so they don't worry, and it's been a while. I also have a post address in Fairfield so my mail goes there. I'll stop and exchange our mail. It's been a few weeks, so I'm sure what's waiting for me is old news, but I'd like to check it nonetheless."

"That sounds like a plan." She sat straighter in the seat.

"Glad you agree." He threw a teasing grin her way.

She crossed her arms. "I've been most agreeable the entire time we've been together."

"Whoa." The horse slowed. "Not ye, Bear. That was for Miss Baker. No need to get defensive, lass. I was jesting. You're awfully serious today. Are ye sure you're all right?"

In typical Sarah fashion, she ignored his question and asked one of her own. "Do you ever go to church, Alex?"

He gripped the reins tight and Bear slowed. Alex adjusted his hold while searching for the right answer. His answer mattered, or she wouldn't have asked, and he had to get it right. *Lord, provide the right words to come out of my mouth.* "Aye, I do. Why do ye ask?"

"I was curious. You haven't mentioned church, yet you pray and talk about the Lord all the time. I guess I'm a little homesick. It feels odd to not be going to church today. It is Sunday, isn't it?"

His heart cheered at her question. He thought out his words before responding. *Lord, help me along here.* "Aye, it's Sunday. However, God doesn't want to interact with you only on Sunday. He wants you to seek him every day."

She tilted her head. "Do you seek him *every* day? I think I know the answer but had to ask."

"I do," he said. He regularly asked God what to do in situations and prayed for others.

"How? Besides a prayer at meal times."

"Aye, they don't call it quiet time for nothing. I haven't been trying to hide it from you, lass. I do rise before you to read my Bible and pray. I also write in my prayer journal most nights."

"So that's the book you're writing in. I wasn't sure. I thought it had to do with tracking sales."

"Aye. I do that as well." His chest vibrated with the low chuckle that escaped. "I have more than one book. The special one—that's the prayer journal—I started on me journey here. It's kept me from being lonely and has drawn me closer to God.

She grew quiet. "Would you read the Bible with me?"

Alex tried to contain his smile but failed. "Sarah, I would love nothing better than to read the Bible with ye. And since ye asked about church, there's a visiting preaching circuit we're headed for. We can worship God with others, hear a few speakers share a message in a tent just as if we were in a church building." She didn't need to know he would be one of the speakers. Not yet, anyway.

"You said it would be like a church service?"

"Aye, lass. Just a little longer since it's an all-day affair."

She smiled. "I think I can handle that. How far away is it?"

"We have a couple days' ride to get there."

"That long?" She scrunched her face.

Alex called it her cute pout face. "You'll be fine. Look how far you've come already."

She bit her lip. "I have adapted quite well, haven't I?" Her special smile appeared.

He grinned back. "Aye, lassie."

She faced forward and placed her hands in her lap. Not gripping the bench board. Not holding her stomach. It was as if her inner peace had calmed her entire system.

They traveled in companionable silence for the next few hours, and Alex enjoyed every minute of it. Back home there was always an expected response because of his role and title. Someone asking him every fifteen minutes if he needed anything. All he ever wanted was to be left alone. Fend for himself. And for some reason, he felt more himself each day Sarah was with him.

How many days did they have left together? He wished it could be a lifetime.

Thirteen

I'm not sure I will enjoy this job anymore after Miss Baker and I part ways. Her presence has changed everything.

—From the journal of Alex Sinclair

For the next few hours, the landscape didn't change much. Trees, wildflowers, and bushes with rolling hills in the distance blurred together as they passed them by. Out of habit, Sarah searched for places to run to if she needed to stop, but the urge never appeared. It was as if the peace from praying affected her entire body and cured the motion sickness. And she was grateful.

Bear's hooves clomped as he pulled the wagon along the dirt road. The rhythm gave Sarah something else to focus on. She watched his black tail flutter from his swift movements. He was a beautiful boy, strong and sturdy. Alex had said he'd had Bear since he was a teen. How did he have the funds for such great stock? Did she dare ask?

Soon a creek appeared, and Alex pulled them to a stop.

"Let's take a dinner break. Bear can drink and rest, and we can write our letters." He tied the reins, jumped down, and went to unharness Bear.

Sarah climbed down and approached Bear's other side to help.

After staking him near the water, they opened the back of the wagon. Sarah took out the hamper they had packed that morning and found a nearby spot to lay the blanket under a shade tree.

Alex climbed inside. "I have an old writing desk we can use as a solid surface." He appeared with the small desk, along with paper, quills, and an inkwell, and lowered it onto the blanket next to the hamper.

Sarah took one look and knew the container and desk were family heirlooms. Another piece of Alex's puzzle she hadn't figured out, and information he did not volunteer.

Sarah opened the hamper and handed Alex the napkin holding the bread and meat she wrapped earlier.

"Thank you, lass." He waited for her.

She picked up her own sandwich.

He grasped her hand. "Let's say a blessing first. Lord, thank you for your protection during our travels. Only you know what lays ahead of us. May your blessings abound. Both with this food and our travels. Amen."

"Amen," Sarah joined in.

While they ate, she soaked in the fresh air, the trickling water, and the birds chirping in the trees. It was as if they were on a picnic, and a pang of home hit Sarah square in the chest. They'd had picnics on a regular basis on the Taylor ranch. Or they once did. It had been a while. Her chest ached as she continued to mourn her past.

When they were finished with their food, Alex handed her the desk and showed her how to use his set of writing tools.

She dipped the quill in the ink and poised her hand, but no words came. How should she tell her brother? Had Luke written to him already? Would he even understand? She wanted to tell him she was safe and not to worry. Maybe that was where she should start.

> *Dear Will,*
>
> *I hope this letter finds you well. You probably have heard from Luke by now and know I left Washton. I won't get into the reasons here. Just know I'm safe and I'm happy.*

Was she happy? What did happiness feel like? She had been cheerful as a young girl on the Taylor farm, before sickness and death had changed things, but also sad after losing her parents and their home. She had found a way to go on back then. Like she was now. But this happy felt different. The peace she'd experienced made her happy. And that was God.

She peeked at the man resting on the blanket beside her.

Her heart flipped. There was something about being with Alex that made her happy as well. He noticed her. Listened. Showed he cared in small ways. He looked after her without smothering her. But with him, it wasn't happiness per say. So what was it?

> *My actions likely upset you, but I believe this was unavoidable for many reasons. I can explain when I see you next. I am not upset, mad, or being rebellious. I didn't have any other way to move forward. Please forgive me if my leaving troubled you or caused grief for you as a pastor. I will write again soon.*
>
> *Your Loving Sister,*
> *Sarah*

Sarah blew the ink dry and folded the parchment. She didn't know when she would see him again. Hopefully soon.

She raised her letter into the air. "I'm finished."

Alex sat up. "Grand. I'll write mine and then we can head oot on the road again."

The practiced ease of how he set up his paper and wrote told of years of experience. "Who are you writing to?"

"My mother and father." Alex bent over the desk and continued his letter. He had elegant handwriting for a man.

"Where are they?" Maybe she could gather some new information.

"In Scotland." He didn't say anything else.

"That's far away. Do you miss them? Plan to go back?"

He glanced up and smiled. "Lass, if you want me to complete my letter, stop asking questions."

She bit her lip. He didn't answer any of them. Why not?

Alex wrote a few more lines. When he stopped, he blew on the ink, put the cap on the inkwell, and packed up all the pieces. "That's done. Ready to go? We have a few more hours to travel before we stop for the night."

Sarah glanced around and nodded. "This was a pretty place to rest. Thanks for letting me write my letter." She stood and folded the blanket while Alex packed the other items.

He nodded but didn't say more before he went to secure Bear to the wagon.

She climbed to her side of the bench and waited.

As he pulled himself onto his side of the seat, he glanced at her but his eyes didn't quite meet hers. He flipped the reins. "Hiya."

What was he hiding?

* * *

ALEX GRIPPED THE REINS TIGHT. He hadn't known how to answer Sarah's questions. He had two sets of voices rattling in his brain—the answers he *should* give and the answers he *wanted* to give. If he said anything, he was afraid the entire truth would come out, and he wasn't ready to explain something he didn't understand himself. The commitment he'd made five years ago didn't seem real. What he desired with Sarah did. What would it be to completely break away from his family? Could he do it? Did he have enough to offer without his inheritance?

The turmoil caused his stomach to mince the food he'd eaten. If he wasn't careful, he'd be the one needing to pull over and run to a bush.

He glanced Sarah's way. Tension radiated from her, and he didn't know how to bring back the peace she exuded before they stopped for their meal.

"Lass." He had to say something.

She eyed him with hurt in her gaze.

"I'm sorry for ignoring your questions. I heard them. I ... I ... don't know how to answer them."

"That would've been an answer. You've been forthright with me about my answers and decisions. Holding my feet to the fire to deal with my emotions to help me figure out what I'm doing. Why can't I do the same for you?"

He forced an uncomfortable chuckle. Anything to make the conversation lighter. "If ye only knew how much you've already done that for me. I'm seeing life, *my* life, in a different way since you've been along. But I'm not sure what to do with all of these new emotions yet, ye ken?"

She nodded. "I do. I've been with you less than a week, but I've learned so much about myself." She met his gaze full on. "You've been on your own for years. You should know yourself by now. Why is it so hard?"

"Aye, lass. I do. But there are complications from my past I will need to deal with. Someday." When he'd have to step into his role as Lord Berrymin and walk away from the anonymity he'd created here in California. It wasn't what he wanted, but it was what was expected of him.

Alex didn't say more. He studied the sky and the terrain. "We have a few more hours till we reach Fairfield. You holding up okay?" A larger city, Fairfield was not a place he wanted Sarah and him to be seen together. If they stopped outside of town for the night, they could arrive first thing in the morning before the streets became crowded. Then continue to the community of Bridgeport. Small enough to not yet have a post office, it was near where the revival was to take place.

"Aye." She mimicked his brogue.

He laughed. A genuine one this time.

She grinned as she faced forward again. "How did you hear about this large church gathering?"

Thankful she spoke with him again, he grabbed onto the topic. "Aye, it's amazing how the act of sitting around a campfire helps spread news. Since I travel from place to place, I bring news I hear with me. As do the people I meet. I like to know things. And I've made friends with circuit preachers in the area." He paused. "Wait. Where is yer brother attending seminary?"

"Someplace called St. Augustine."

"The new missionary college? Did ye know that's in Benicia? We're heading that way. Many of the students from there will be participating in the event." Which meant the chances of running into her brother were high. Good for Sarah. Not so good for Alex.

The subtle movement of his wrists directed Bear around another bend. Because he cut off the main stagecoach route, they traveled along a narrow path with large rocks and trees to navigate. The bumps and movement caused Sarah to slide into him, and the contact did all sorts of things to his insides. An unexpected rut had him placing his arm around her to prevent her from falling off the bench. How he desired her to stay near his side. Her green eyes went wide when he glanced her way. "You okay?"

"Yes, forgive me for bumping into you." She wiggled away from him but the rattling caused her to smack into him again.

"There's nothing to forgive. These roads are bumpy. I'm lucky I'm holding my seat."

She glanced behind them as the wagon tilted.

He smiled at her. "She'll hold. Been through worse."

She frowned. "It sounds like the wood will snap."

"The biggest issue we could face is another broken wheel. And there's nothing to be done about it to prevent that from happening. It's just the way traveling is."

"You've invested a lot in your wagon. I don't want anything to happen to it."

"Aye. But I also trust God to provide. His ways are better than me own. I can't go out in the world fearful of things going wrong." An interesting choice of words as he fretted over his future and saying goodbye to Sarah.

She crossed her arms, her hands grasping her upper arms.

"Are you cold, lass? Maybe we should stop soon."

She shook her head. "No. I was just looking around and realizing how much out in the middle of nowhere we were."

"God's beautiful landscape, isn't it?" he asked.

"I guess. It's different after being near that wagon train last night. I didn't realize how much I missed people."

His jaw dropped. "Are you saying you're tired of me?"

She laughed as he'd intended. "Nae."

He placed his hand on her shoulder. "I promise you'll be safe, lass. I won't let anything happen to ye."

"But what if something happens to ye?"

He paused before answering. She was worried about him? "What's got you so fearful?"

Sarah gripped the side of the bench, waiting for the bend to straighten out. "I've had something happen to everyone I care about. My parents. Michael."

"Are you saying you care about me, lass?" He sent her a cheeky grin.

Her face grew scarlet.

He reached out and held her hand. "Don't be embarrassed, Sarah. I care for ye too. We've become friends on this journey. I think we make a good team. Don't ye?"

She shrugged.

"Lass." He placed his fingers under her chin. "If this scares ye, we can stop right now or keep driving till we find others to set up camp next to." Although he didn't think they'd find anyone close by, even though they weren't far from Fairfield.

Her face looked glum.

He pulled on the reins. "Let's set up camp for the night. We don't have much farther to go, and it will be easier to drive on the road in fresh daylight tomorrow."

Fourteen

—From the journal of Alex Sinclair

Sarah sipped her second cup of coffee after eating a larger than normal breakfast. They had risen a little later than usual, in order to wait for the post office to open, which was a nice change.

Many words went unsaid last night, but Sarah wasn't worried. They had time. One thing was for certain. She enjoyed these quiet moments with Alex. They had both grown since that rainy night she first joined him. No longer did she feel stuck. Instead, there was peace and anticipation. The Bible verses Alex read across the campfire last night echoed in her mind. She closed her eyes. *Lord. I don't know what you have planned for me. But I'm ready and willing.*

She opened her eyes to find Alex's watching her.

"Praying?" His head tilted to the side while he held his tin cup to his mouth. The joy in his gaze warmed her heart.

She nodded. "The desire to speak to God bubbled up, and I didn't want to ignore it." She loved that she could share her innermost thoughts with him.

"Aye. That's good, lass. Very good. Ye ready to pack up?"

"Ready as I'll ever be." The letter to her brother burned in her pocket. She bit her lip, wondering how he would handle the news it brought.

"How's the leg this morning?" He lifted the crates and carried them to the wagon.

She stood. A twinge of pain was all that was left in her leg. "Stiff, but not much more than that. It's a relief not to worry about it."

"Aye." Alex followed her to her side of the bench seat and held out his hand.

She placed hers in his and allowed him to lift her. Heat radiated through her body.

He winked at her before he ran around Bear and climbed in on his own side. As they drove closer to town, Sarah wondered if Fairfield would look any different than Washton.

"Washton's post office burnt down years ago, and the government decided not to replace it. Our mail goes to the store instead. Is the post an actual office here or at a store?"

"An actual office. Bridgeport, where we head next, doesn't have a post office yet, so that's why we're stopping here." Alex pulled into an empty lot behind the livery and jumped down from the seat. "We'll park here."

Sarah held onto the side as she lowered herself to the ground. She straightened her skirt before Alex approached, having given instructions to the young stable lad on what to do with Bear.

His bright blue eyes turned stormy. "You're not going to like this, lass, but I need ye to step inside the wagon and hide while we're here."

She grew light-headed.

"We can't pretend here. People know me. It would make things …" He glanced away before meeting her gaze again. "… difficult for both of us."

Lord, this wasn't what I had in mind when I prayed earlier. Yet Alex hadn't steered her wrong, and she trusted him. She nodded. "I don't want to cause you any headaches." She had forgotten, in the eyes of many they were sinning, even though Alex had been a perfect gentleman. The people from the wagon train hadn't known them and believed them to be married. If people knew him here, they would know he didn't have a wife and would ask questions.

They walked to the back of the wagon, and he lifted her into the darkened space. At least it wasn't mid-day yet, when the inside would be too warm all closed off.

"I'll be quick as a roadrunner. In and out. And Sarah?"

She looked out the back from where he stood. "Yes?"

"Thank ye for understanding. I'm sorry, lass."

She lowered herself onto the floor of the wagon as he closed the flap. She didn't know if he was sorry for closing her inside or for something else. It was the something else that worried her.

* * *

ALEX STRODE around the livery onto the main street. He hoped she would listen and stay in the wagon. He didn't like leaving her. But he didn't have much choice. Her reputation would be ruined, and he couldn't offer for her. In his heart and in the eyes of the Lord, he was doing nothing wrong. In fact, after their conversation about church and reading the Bible, he understood why God had put her in his path.

Still, driving into a town where someone could recognize

him would be a problem. Even if they saw her riding alongside him or walking with him down the street.

He pushed his hat forward on his head. Guilt laced through him, knowing she didn't deserve to be hidden away. She should be able to enjoy window shopping and visiting a new place. And he would love to have her on his arm. But he couldn't take a chance. Not here.

His boots clanked along the wooden walkway as he headed straight for the post office. He'd be quick. But as soon as that thought played in his mind, he recognized the two men headed straight for him.

"Hiya, Alex." The taller of the two waved his hand high.

"Halo, Wes. Robert." Alex reached for the door of the post office, hoping the hint would move them along.

"Been a while since we've seen you. How ya been?" Wes grabbed the door and held it open.

Alex didn't want to, but he couldn't be rude. "Aye, great. How are things with ye?"

Robert shook his head. "Well, if truth be known—"

Normally he would take the time to fully engage, but he couldn't leave Sarah for long. Nor did he want to.

"So what do you think?" Robert looked at him with an eagerness in his eyes.

Alex blinked and realized he hadn't heard a single word. Not wanting to take more precious time away from his mission, he told them the truth. "I'm sorry. I'm in a hurry. The only thing that I ask myself is 'have you prayed about it? What is God telling you to do?'"

Not waiting for a reply, he entered the building and released his breath when they didn't follow him inside.

"Well, if it isn't Alex Smith." The postmaster stood behind the counter.

"Halo, Paul." Alex pulled off his hat. He knew the

postmaster well, since he was one of the first friends Alex had made when he came to California. And he was the only one who knew of Alex's true background.

Paul waved an envelope in the air. "Your timing is excellent, as always."

His gut clenched. What news was waiting for him. Had something happened to his mother or father?

He placed his and Sarah's letters on the counter. "I have letters I need to mail as well."

Paul slid a stack of letters toward Alex.

"A whole stack?" Why were there so many?

Paul placed his hand on the pile. "I think you should read them right away."

Alex's hand froze as he reached for the mail. "What makes you say that?"

Paul shrugged. "You've received three different letters from Scotland. Usually, you only receive one every few months. Either there's a lot of news, or they are trying to reach you. As it takes time to arrive from Scotland, the news may be old, but it looks important. One even says 'rush.'"

Alex picked up the pile and scrolled through the letters. Two were written in his mother's elegant hand. The third was unfamiliar, but definitely female. One of his mother's was thicker than the other, so there was most likely more than one note inside. "Thanks for holding these for me."

"Not a problem. When do you think you'll be back again?"

"A few weeks? I'm not sure." He hadn't given much thought to his plans after the prayer revival.

"You know you could settle here." Paul's encouraging smile warmed Alex's heart.

He'd have a friend if he did decide to settle here. But was this where he wanted to put down roots? With all the places he'd been, there were three communities he'd consider. This was one of them. But he wasn't ready to settle yet. He liked the traveling and serving aspects of what he did. And now having someone with him. Someone with red hair and green eyes, who laughed and craved adventure, just like him. Didn't complain when things got hard. He couldn't picture Rebecca doing that, although he couldn't picture Rebecca at all. She was only ten years old when he left.

He strode to the bench seat in the corner and sat. The first letter he opened was from his mother. As he unfolded the parchment it held only three lines. He scanned the words on the page and then again. They didn't make any sense. He opened her other letter. Three sheets fell out of the envelope. The first one he picked up was his mother's. Much more detailed. As he read, a giant sense of unease filled his stomach. His mother was concerned and wanted him to do something about the scandal unfolding. Blamed his absence for the situation. But he couldn't figure out the entire circumstance with her cryptic words. What did she expect him to do when he was an ocean away?

"Are you okay?" a familiar voice asked.

Lost in the letter, he raised his head and blinked. Beautiful green eyes filled with warmth and concern sent his heart racing in a different direction. "I'm not sure."

"You look as if you've received bad news." She sat on the bench beside him, unaware of how familiar it would appear.

He shook his head. "I'm not sure yet how to interpret what's in here."

"That sounds baffling. Care to talk about it?"

No. He really didn't want to talk about it. Doing so would mean revealing everything, and he didn't know if that was a good idea or not. He looked at his traveling companion and something dawned on him. "You're not supposed to be here. You couldn't heed one simple request."

"It's not that. It's—"

"Nae. We need to go, lass." He cut her off because no matter what she said, she hadn't listened. He folded the letters and shoved them into his pocket. They could not be found together.

He liked Sarah, would love to marry her in fact, but family obligations made that option impossible. Given that, he couldn't protect her with them out in the open.

He was at fault. There was so much Sarah didn't understand. All because he hadn't revealed his true identity.

He glanced at the front desk where Paul stood and watched, his brow furrowed.

Not realizing the scrutiny they attracted by sitting together, Sarah's full attention remained on Alex. "But your news. Do you need to write another letter?"

The door opened and a man entered. He walked to the counter, where he asked Paul a question. There was something in his hand he showed Paul.

"Nae." Was all Alex could say.

It was too late. He knew it in his heart.

Paul pointed to Alex and Sarah. The man rotated, and his eyes widened.

Fifteen

Sometimes we are placed in a situation where we have no control, and we must fully lean on you, Lord. This is one of those times. Guide me and show me your way.

—From the journal of Alex Sinclair

"Sarah! Oh, praise God, I've found you. I was afraid I wouldn't."

Sarah froze. She hadn't noticed the man enter, but she recognized the voice and watched Alex's shoulders slump. In that split-second, she knew Alex had been right. She should've stayed in the wagon. Their time together was over. She turned.

Her brother Will raced toward her, swooped down, and picked her up right off the bench. He smashed her face against his chest, his hug so tight she couldn't breathe.

"Will? Is it really you?" She was breathless. "Put me down. I can't inhale."

He set her down but didn't remove his hands from her

waist. "Where have you been? I've been worried sick about you." His hands cupped her face.

"Will."

"Were you kidnapped?" He didn't stop to breathe, but barreled on, his gaze darting to Alex and back to her.

"Will."

"Why did you leave? I've been so worried."

"Will!"

He stopped. "What?" His gaze searched hers. His eyes filled with unshed tears. And love.

"I left on my own. I'm safe. I ... I just wrote you a letter." Sarah waved her arm toward the counter.

Movement behind her had her glancing at Alex as he stood and stepped toward them. This was not how she wanted to introduce him to her brother. "I already mailed it, lass, but I can ask Paul to pull it out if ye want me to."

"Who's this?" Will demanded, his shout loud enough to draw attention from both the attendant and the patron he was helping.

Sarah worried he might yell at her too.

"We should talk somewhere private," said Alex, his voice quiet. "We dinnae want others to hear our conversation."

The attendant came out of nowhere and handed Alex a key. "Use my place. You know where it is."

He nodded. "Thanks, Paul."

The man didn't say anything, just strode back to his position behind the counter.

"Shall we?" Alex led them outside and down the street a few blocks before turning onto another street.

No one spoke. Only the uneven tapping of their shoes hitting the path filled the air. Alex led the way with Will plodding along next to her. The sound had no rhythm. Out of alignment. Which was exactly how she felt with both of them.

She wished she was five again and able to throw a temper tantrum to change the atmosphere.

"Have you been with him this entire time? Do you know what that looks like, what that means?"

"He saved me from a horrible situation. And he's been a perfect gentleman," she hissed.

Will released a false laugh. "I bet."

Alex glanced over his shoulder. He didn't make eye contact, and his face was pale. He didn't attempt to defend himself, even though he must've heard every word.

"It's not like that at all."

Will studied her. "Are you truly okay? I was so worried when Luke sent the telegram. I've been looking for you. Wondering if you would try to find me."

Sarah wasn't sure how to answer. She hadn't known where Will was and never thought she could find him, or that he'd want her to. But based on his reaction, he cared. And that filled some of the hole in her heart. A part of her wished she could go back and do things differently. Being on the road this past week had given her a fresh perspective. Her heart thumped. But if she hadn't left as she did, she wouldn't have met Alex or had the time to find herself. To find God and his peace after all that had happened.

Alex turned down an alley and into a small courtyard. He must've been here before because he strode to the third door on the right and inserted the key. He held it open, glanced at her, and spoke in a monotone voice. "After you."

Sarah hesitated, but Will pressed his hands into her back and pushed her over the threshold. When she stopped, he stopped next to her. Alex closed the door and completed their circle. Her gaze locked with his before she glanced at Will.

Will looked madder than Old Fred, Luke's bull.

The urge to run again filled her.

* * *

Alex was thankful Sarah's brother cared enough to have this conversation. He didn't worry about himself so much, but Sarah. It was obvious her brother loved her and traveled quite a distance to search for her.

Sarah didn't wait. She cleared her throat. "Will, this is Mr. Alex Smith. Mr. Smith, this is my brother, William Baker."

If she wanted control of the situation, Alex would follow her lead. He held out his hand and held his breath. "Pleasure to meet you."

Will gripped it hard and shook. Stared straight into Alex's eyes. Years of scrutiny from his father made it easy for Alex not to react.

"Your accent. Where are you from, Mr. Smith?"

Alex flexed his hand when Will let go. "Scotland."

"Didn't know the name Smith was a Scottish name."

"Will," Sarah pleaded.

"It's okay, lass." Alex wavered for a moment. "My full name is Alexander Sinclair."

Will gritted his teeth. Glanced at his sister. "Did you know his real name?"

Alex peered at her.

She stood with her mouth agape. The hurt in her eyes broke Alex in two. She swallowed. "Was everything else you told me a lie, as well?"

"What has happened between you two?" Will's question echoed around the room.

Alex and Sarah stared at each other. Her green eyes flashed.

"Answer me, Sarah. Do I need to perform a marriage ceremony? You've been with this man overnight. What is going on?"

"Nothing," Alex and Sarah answered at the same time.

"I have eyes and can see how you're both behaving. This isn't nothing. Please explain before we return to Washton."

Sarah flinched, then faced her brother. "I am not going. Back. To. Washton." She leaned closer. "Ever."

A deep V formed between Will's eyebrows. "What happened with Luke, Sarah? He's hurt. And so are Caroline and Rose. Do you have any idea what your leaving has done to them?"

Sarah toed the floor with her boot.

Alex knew she had indeed thought about her actions that night because they'd discussed it. But she had to explain her reasons in a way her brother would understand. *Lord, give him an open mind.* It was obvious Will cared for his sister and wouldn't force her to do anything, but explanations needed to be aired.

When no one said anything, the desire to speak filled Alex. But he had to be cautious. He had his own family and whatever was happening back home to consider. He cleared his throat. "If I could help explain?"

Both siblings looked at him, their red-hair matching, but their eye color different. A pang of homesickness overcame him at seeing their resemblance. He missed his siblings.

He didn't have time to explore those emotions right now. "Your sister approached me late one night as I was preparing to leave town." He held up his hand. "No, Sarah, please don't interrupt."

She crossed her arms in front of her and tapped her foot while her brother crossed his arms and growled. If the conversation wasn't so serious, he would've poked fun at the similarity in their stances.

"It was raining. She had a suitcase and determination on her face." He glanced at Will. "She can be quite stubborn, you ken."

Will shuffled his feet. "You don't have to tell me that."

Alex thought he heard a humph come from Sarah but didn't acknowledge it.

"I had no idea what she was running from. In my travels I see all sorts of situations. Women who are treated harsh. Children who have gone without food. The fear in her eyes was what I reacted to. I wasn't going to leave her with no place to go."

"But she rode away with you. In a wagon. By herself. Propriety—"

"I know, I know." Alex raised his hands. Placed his feet farther apart to hold himself up. *Lord, help me here.* "I promise nothing untoward has occurred. It would've been worse to leave her there. And we've been careful who has seen her." He glanced at Sarah. There was one more piece of information he had to share. He swallowed. This was not how he wanted her to find out. He kept his gaze on Sarah. "I understand propriety more than ye know. It's been drilled into me since birth. Ye see, my father is the Earl of Debear. I am known as Lord Berrymin."

Sarah's eyes widened. Her lip quivered.

Alex glanced at Will. His face had lost its color. This was why he kept his identity a secret.

All three studied one another. The only sound were the gasps coming from Sarah as realization dawned.

Alex wished he had told her the other night, when he had more time to explain. But he had wanted more time in the dream they had created for themselves. There was hadn't been a need to rush and change everything.

Sarah placed her hand over her mouth and turned away.

Her hunched shoulders shot an arrow through Alex's heart.

Will cleared his throat. "Nobility, huh?"

Sarah lifted her head and peered over her shoulder. "Lord Berrymin, Bear. Your horse is named after you?"

He'd never felt so foolish in his life. "Aye, I did name my horse Berrymin." He shook his head. "But I don't use Lord Berrymin here."

Sarah raised her eyebrows. "Why not?"

Will placed his hand on her shoulder. "Sarah, before you go asking the wrong questions, let's let the man explain." He glared at Alex. "I've read why nobility come to the states. What I don't understand is why you chose Sarah. We don't have money to save a crumbling estate. Or connections to others of the same birth. Were you using her? I've seen men of nobility take advantage of people. Yet display an odd sense of honor once caught. I want to know why you haven't offered to marry Sarah already."

Sixteen

Life can be full of difficult choices. Things don't always go the way we want them to. But your ways, Lord, are always perfect. I'm writing Isaiah 55:8 here to remind me. 'For my thoughts are not your thoughts, neither are your ways my ways, saith the Lord'. I'm trusting in you, Lord.

—From the journal of Alex Sinclair

Heat crawled up Sarah's neck. How had she landed right back where she started? She wanted to marry Alex, more than anything, but not like this. Not as a decision made for her. Never again.

She opened her mouth, but Alex shot her a look. She bit her lip.

He shook his head. "Nae, Will. I cannot marry Sarah." He hesitated, then met her gaze. "Because I'm already spoken for."

What? Sarah stepped back, her heart in her throat. She swayed as the blood drained out of her head. Her stomach churned the same way it did when she first rode on the wagon bench. It would serve Alex right if she had to use his shoes as a bush.

Will's face reddened. "So you dally with my sister because you don't have to be responsible? Sarah, did you have no consideration of your reputation?"

Alex put his hands on his hips. "I didn't *dally* with your sister. And your sister has been responsible. Mature in her actions. Ye should be quite proud of her. It took a lot of courage to do what she did."

Will threw up his hands. "You haven't had one run away with a grown man."

Sarah moved between the two of them, but Alex blocked her with his arm. "Nae, I haven't. I have young sisters myself, and I know how I would want them to be treated. And the moral code I live by." He sighed. "As a servant of Jesus Christ. Not all men do."

At this, Will crossed his arms and narrowed his eyes. "Explain yourself."

Sarah swallowed. Her dry mouth took a bit to function. But she didn't want the two men she cared for to argue. It wouldn't change anything. She stepped between them. "You don't have to explain anything, Alex."

"Do not defend him." Will sought out Alex over her head. "Go on. I want to know what you mean."

Alex sighed. "I'm a Christian. Like ye. I came here to serve. I couldn't serve back home because everyone knows who I am. My father agreed I could come here to work and raise funds to establish land for our family. But I haven't saved much. I keep giving it away."

Pieces clicked together for Sarah. "You could afford to sell the woman and her children the toys at no profit."

He nodded. "Most people don't want a handout. But they dinnae have enough funds either. I travel with my peddler wagon, selling wares to those who can afford them and those who can't."

"What will you do when your family finds out you haven't bought any land?" Sarah asked.

Alex shook his head. "Ah dinnae ken. I have three more years before my betrothed can marry." He looked at Sarah sheepishly. "She's ten years younger than me. I left when I was twenty. I couldn't handle watching my future bride grow up alongside my sisters. I would have a difficult time being her husband." He looked at Will. "Do ye understand?"

Recognition dawned. Sarah placed her hand at her mouth. "You have an arranged marriage."

He nodded.

She held her head high as she stepped away from their circle. Blinked away the wetness forming behind her eyes. Anything to not show how much this hurt. Alex was unattainable. Her heart couldn't process this information. She snuck a glance at his face. Wanted to read remorse or disappointment there. Anything.

He looked away, his face pale. A tear dripped down his cheek.

Her heart didn't fall completely apart. Even though she felt betrayed, neither of them ever made a promise. Talked about the future. Led the other on. If she was honest with herself, the hope of a future with Alex was all in her head. How her mind and heart had thought ... the conflict that warred within her made understand her feelings a challenge. Should she be angry or hurt?

She cared for Alex. Had learned his true heart, or what she thought was true. She didn't think he could hide that. He was honoring commitments to his family and betrothed and did not toy with her in the way other men might have. Of course, he was gone from her forever, and that left a bruise on her already battered heart. What did the future hold now?

Alex wiped a hand down his face. He looked as if a wind and rainstorm had caught him unaware. "I withheld this information because I didn't want to be treated different. Being a member of the peerage can cause people to behave oddly. Look at both of yer responses. I wanted people to know Alex, not Lord Berrymin. I needed to find out who I was. Much like ye, Sarah. You were tired of decisions being made for ye and wanted the freedom to make your own choices."

Will frowned at her. "Is this true?"

She opened her mouth. Closed it again.

"Aye. Tell him the truth, lass. All of it," Alex encouraged.

Sarah moved to the small wooden table and sat in one of the chairs. Her fingers tapped on the wood as she searched for the words. "You left. Michael got sick. It was heartbreaking losing him. But there wasn't time to grieve. Then Luke's ma got sick, and there was so much to do." Her eyes caught both men watching her. "Um. Well, the night before ma died, she pleaded with Luke to marry me. Said it wouldn't look right with us under the same roof. Didn't matter that the girls were there and Jimmy. Luke promised. When she passed, he declared we'd wed the next day. I left that night." She pleaded, "I couldn't, Will. It wouldn't have been right. Luke never asked me what I wanted. There were too many emotions to deal with to add marriage and motherhood into the mix within a twenty-four hour timeframe. We needed time to grieve. To figure out things. And to find God amongst our pain and sorrow."

Her brother knelt. "And?"

"I have found God again. I know I left abruptly, and it was rather rude of me." Tears streamed down her face. She paused, hoping Will would say something to counter her words.

After a while he whispered, "Keep going. Don't let me stop you."

She tried to narrow her eyes at him, but based on his grin, she didn't succeed. She grew serious. "I don't want to live in Washton. There isn't anything there for me."

"I'll be there." Will stood.

Sarah's gaze followed him. "You will? When?"

He sighed. "When I get done figuring out what to do with you. I'm supposed to take over the church there."

"Oh, that's wonderful, Will." She was truly happy for him.

He placed his hands on his hips. "It sure is. But I have to somehow explain why my wayward sister ran away in the middle of the night and who she was with."

"Oh." The conversation with Alex her first night on the trail played in her mind. She glanced at her brother and winced.

"Exactly." Will paced the floor.

Alex cleared his throat. "You're all done with your studies, then?"

Will looked at her. "You told him about me?"

Alex cleared his throat. "She talked about ye quite a bit."

Will swiveled to face Alex. "Oh? What did she say? Did she call me a brute?" He crossed his arms, but he had a smirk on his face.

Alex leaned toward Will. "She said ye were the only family she had left, and when you went away she had a great big hole in her heart. She loves you and hopes you loved her enough to understand. She didn't intend to hurt you."

An odd gleam entered Will's eyes. He swallowed. Closed his eyes. Then shuffled over to her and knelt beside her chair. "I'm sorry, Sarah."

She pushed into his arms, thankful to clear the air.

"You silly goat." He talked into her hair. "I love you, and I do understand. I just wish you contacted me or tried to explain to Luke instead of running away."

Sarah couldn't stop the tears as she sobbed into Will's collar. His big arms encircled her and made her feel safe and secure. How she had missed him.

He released his hold. "You know you're going to have to come with me now."

She nodded but didn't look at Alex. She couldn't. All her emotions were so raw. She'd miss him. She would remember this past week fondly. But her adventure was over. A white handkerchief appeared in her hand, and she wiped her tears. She went to hand it back to Alex.

"Keep it, lass," he said.

She gazed into his eyes. "Thank you." New tears flowed down her cheeks.

He swallowed. His eyes shone like glass. He faced Will. "Take care of her." He reached a hand out.

Will hesitated, then placed his hand in Alex's. "Thank you. I'll take it from here." He took her hand and led her out the door.

She didn't look back. She couldn't. With each step she and Will took, the distance between her and Alex grew. She clutched Will's hand, his presence the one light guiding her. It was over. The wagon, the long talks, the accent—all gone. And along with those things, a piece of her heart.

* * *

ALEX FLINCHED when the door closed. No formal goodbye. His heart ached knowing he wouldn't see her again. He also rejoiced she was reunited with her brother. Relieved she knew the truth about him as well. Although he yearned to hear her thoughts on the matter.

Paul's house was eerily quiet. He stood in the middle of the kitchen, wanting to go after her but knowing he couldn't. She wasn't his responsibility any longer. But he cared. And her absence extinguished a bright light in his world.

He patted his jacket for the letters he'd received. They screamed to be read, so he sat at the kitchen table and pulled them out. He opened his youngest sister's letter.

She shared about her new horse and how much the mare looked like Bear. That her riding was improving, and she couldn't wait to ride with him around the property. He missed the little sprite. She would be eleven now, the view of her world expanding with each passing year.

The second letter was from his sister Samantha. It was full of young lady terms Alex didn't understand. The dreaminess of her descriptions caused him to itch as he tried to interpret what was being said. Samantha was the same age as his betrothed. Both fifteen and dear friends. If there was one consolation to marrying the young girl, he liked the idea of his wife and sisters being friends.

Her slanted script reflected the tale of how both girls had learned cotillion dances and attended the local assembly. She mentioned the handsome boys they'd met and all the fun they had interacting with these men.

Alex snorted. *Men.* At fifteen. It was hard to believe his little Sam was interested in boys. For the first time he wished he was there so he could watch over her. Although his parents were most likely keeping an eye on things.

He read further, and Samantha shared another story about a specific boy and how he paid particular attention to her friend. An odd sensation curled through him. It wasn't until he reread the line again that he realized the *friend* must be Rebecca. *His* Rebecca. There wasn't much more, so he didn't know what to make of it.

His mother's letter again beckoned him to read it now that he had read Sam's. She'd filled up an entire sheet and every line was about his future wife making a fool of herself. Her lamentations made clear everyone knew there was a betrothal agreement, yet her behavior showed otherwise.

The itchy sensation grew as Alex thought through the timing and ramifications. Why would Rebecca's parents allow her to behave so? Was this a ploy to bring him back to Scotland? Never did he believe she would cause a scandal. No one did. Would she have done so if he had been there? He pulled at his collar. He didn't mean to cause angst for anyone, especially his parents, but he didn't regret his choices.

In the last part of the letter, his mother chastised him for being absent and unavailable to ensure his future bride did not stray. Curious she used those specific words. The lass was only fifteen. How much trouble could she get into?

He set down his mother's letter and lifted the third envelope off the table. A sour taste flooded his mouth. His hand shook as he broke the seal, unfolded the paper, and read the bold script.

> *Lord Berrymin,*
>
> *I hope this letter finds you well, wherever you are. I suspect you're much happier away from here. I shall be blunt. I have no wish to marry you now or ever. I shall not leave Bruin. It is quite absurd to expect me to wed a man who has not spoken to me in years, despite what my parents think or what is expected of me. You don't know if I prefer butter or marmalade on my toast. The answer, if you must know, is marmalade.*
>
> *I hope you will honor my decision. Do not write to me. Do not return for me. I have made my choice.*
>
> *Lady Rebecca Yount*

Alex reread the letter and didn't know whether to laugh, be mad, or worry about Rebecca's reputation. She possessed a rebellious streak. Between the letters from his mother and sisters, he could guess she wanted to be free to flirt and secure her own beau in a more romantic way than being assigned a husband at the age of ten.

He agreed. If it wasn't for honor, he would've argued against the arrangement from the beginning. But his parents had pleaded and explained the need for the two families to merge. He wondered what both sets of parents would say to her declaration.

Should he go home? Or did he send a response to his parents and ask them to clarify if he was honor bound to marry the lass? Did Rebecca announce her dismissal of him publicly? Did people believe he would accept that type of behavior, even if she was fifteen?

On one hand, she was young. Unable to know the ways of the world. But Sarah was young as well. Four years older than Rebecca. She also had experienced more heartbreak and loss. And had learned how to survive and stand up for herself.

Sweet, honest, fun, adventurous Sarah. Did he dare believe he was free to marry her? It didn't feel true. And did it matter? Her brother wouldn't trust him. Neither may she. And where would he find her? No, he had to move forward. That meant following through with his plan to attend the prayer revival. And wait for the mail to cross the ocean to hear from his parents again.

Seventeen

Change comes whether we are ready for it or not. Many times, it's putting into motion something much bigger than ourselves. All we can do is continue forward while we wait on you, Lord, to reveal your plan.

—From the journal of Alex Sinclair

"You can let go of me. I'm not going to run away." Sarah pulled on her arm as they walked to the livery. She could see Alex's wagon in the back. She would miss it so much.

"I'm happy to have you right here. By my side. I still can't believe you took off like that. With a stranger in the middle of the night. I was so scared for you. Luke was worried about you too."

"He just wanted me to cook, clean, and watch the girls. That's all they needed me for. But I want more than that, Will."

"I'm sure that was not *all* Luke expected of you. You were family to them. We both are. Like a sister."

"You don't marry your sister, Will."

Will stumbled mid-step. Furrowed his brow. Faced her. "You're right." His voice was quiet. "I'm sorry, Sarah."

"I am? You are?" She was prepared to argue more points.

He sighed. "Yes. I'm so used to you being young and needing guidance and direction. But look at you. You're a grown woman. You have your own thoughts and feelings. And it doesn't seem like you've had a chance to share them with anyone."

"Alex listened." She glanced away.

"Who?" he asked.

"Mr. Smith ... er, Mr. Sinclair."

Will stiffened before he grabbed the reins of his saddled horse from the young lad. He handed over a coin, then mounted. He then reached down a hand to Sarah. All while gritting his teeth.

She glanced at her dress. "I'm not dressed for riding. Where are we going?"

Will closed his eyes. "We aren't going far. There's a church revival in the next town. I'm supposed to be there already, so we'll go there before figuring out what's next. I have a blanket you can wrap around your legs. We can get you some new clothes when we get there. Hop up. It will be like old times."

"I'm a little bigger than I was back then."

Will shrugged. "We don't have much choice."

She placed her arm into his hand and he pulled her onto the back of the horse. Her skirts crept up and she took the blanket Will provided and draped it over her legs so it fell on either side, covering her. Her knees gripped the sides of his horse as she wrapped her arms around Will's waist. She didn't mention Alex was headed to the same place. Maybe it was good Will found her here rather than at the revival. Would Alex still go? How big was this event? Her heart fluttered. Would she see him there? Did she want to see him?

Will led his horse to the street. "Hold on tight." He urged his mount into a trot, and they left on the same side streets Alex had taken when they arrived. So much for shopping and exploring a new city. Although she didn't think she'd ever care to visit Fairfield again.

Sarah gripped her wrists to secure herself better and mentally prepared for the jolts of riding.

"How did you ride in a wagon without getting sick? Do you not get motion sick anymore?" Will called out against the pounding of the horse's hooves.

Sarah grimaced. "We had to stop. Several times."

"And he was okay with that?"

"Alex handled it well. After the first day, when I jumped out while we were moving and injured my leg."

"You what?" Will placed a hand on her arms.

"I'm okay. But my leg hurt for a few days. It's probably why he didn't drop me off somewhere. I couldn't do much."

"You felt safe with him?"

"I did. He was kind. And shared God's word with me. Encouraged me to write to you. I think ... I was falling in love with him." She hadn't meant to say it aloud, but the words slipped out before she could stop them. The truth settled in her chest, heavy and bittersweet. She leaned into Will's back. Bit her lip, hard. She would not cry over him.

Her bruised heart ached. She had found someone who understood her. Who liked the same things she did. Connected with her on a level she never had with anyone else. But he had a title. Lord Berrymin. She buried her face deeper as a tear escaped. He'd lived his life in luxury while she grew up on a ranch. Working to survive every single day.

Will squeezed her arm. "I'm sorry, Sarah."

More tears streamed down her cheeks as she clung to her brother. Even though she preferred to ride in the wagon, she was thankful Will couldn't watch her break down. After a few minutes, she looked behind them, but only saw dust clouds. The broken pieces of her heart floating amongst them.

She didn't know what her future held, but her adventure with Alex was over. A part of her heart was left behind with him. And she didn't think she'd ever get it back.

* * *

FOR A LONG WHILE, Alex sat in his friend's kitchen on that wooden chair. He prayed. And prayed some more. God didn't provide answers, but Alex knew those would come in God's timing, if they came at all. He'd lived enough life to have faith. In the meantime, he had a job to do and would follow through with it.

He opened the door and collided with his friend.

"Good. I caught you before you left."

"I'm heading out now." Alex handed Paul the key. "Thank ye for the use of yer place." He searched his friend's face. "And your discretion."

Paul waved his hand. "Don't mention it. I hope you got everything squared away. Not sure where you're headed, but another letter came today. Thought it might be important." He handed Alex the envelope.

"A lot of excitement happening back home, it seems." He forced a laugh, but it came out as a groan. He walked over the threshold holding up the letter. "Thanks again."

Paul motioned back inside. "You're more than welcome to sit and read it here."

"Nae. I need to go if I'm to make my next destination. I'll read it on the trail." He tipped his hat as he strode away. He meandered through the back alleys so as not to run into anyone else.

As he approached the wagon, a sadness engulfed him. The prospect of riding on the bench alone depressed him. She had been with him one week. But what an impact she had made on him and his heart. *Why, God?*

He stomped to the wagon, hoping to shake off the melancholy. He had to cling to hope. To wait for God's answers. He'd harness Bear after he read this next letter from his mother.

He opened the thin envelope and read the first paragraph. Aye. His mother chastised him again for not being there.

> *But maybe your absence is for the best. If you were present, my dear son, Rebecca's true colors may not have shown through. It's not my wish to have such a brazen lady as a daughter-in-law.*

Brazen? He continued reading, dread filling his entire body. When he reached the last line, he froze.

His future bride had indeed caused quite a ruckus. He could only imagine his mother's face when Rebecca made her grand announcement that she would never marry Lord Berrymin.

He grinned. In a way, he was proud of her standing up for herself. In some ways, her situation mirrored Sarah's. She didn't want her husband to be decided for her. But the choice to say no and how she went about it affected more people than herself. He could imagine the discomfort coming from everyone in the room. But all he felt was relief.

Alex let his head fall back, then pressed his palms to his eyes. The contract was broken. He didn't have to marry a young girl who he had nothing in common with. And he was free. Peace swept through him. He knew family duty meant he would follow in his father's footsteps. As heir, it was expected. But after seeing this beautiful country, with God as his companion, he never wanted to go back to that cultured life.

But what now? His father expected him to return to take on the responsibilities of Lord Berrymin of Bruin. Although they had discussed a new plan if he found land here. Could he honor his duty from across the ocean? Would his brother be willing to run things in his stead?

He had to find Sarah. Share his news with her. He dashed over to the stable. "Lad. Can you get the stallion? The one called Bear?"

"Yes, sir. Coming right away, sir." The lad ran into the livery.

Alex paced while his mind raced. He didn't know where they went, but that was okay. Maybe he didn't need to search quite yet. Something nudged him to trust. Besides, he had made a commitment to the prayer gathering and needed to get there first.

The lad steered Bear over to Alex.

Alex tossed him a coin. "Thanks, lad."

"Thank you, sir." The boy grinned and ran away.

Alex led Bear to the front of the wagon, secured him in the harness, and climbed onto the bench seat. He glanced at the open space next to him. His heart ached, but it also contained a mix of hope and expectation. Was that because of his mother's letter or the one person who added color to the world around him?

As he headed away from Fairfield and toward the next town of Bridgeport, anticipation filled him. He couldn't wait to spend time in the word and share his faith with others.

* * *

AFTER A FULL DAY'S RIDE, Sarah and Will reached Bridgeport. As they rode through the small town, she compared the smaller community to Washton, and a pang of homesickness overcame her. They continued through main street to the outskirts of town and beyond, where they came upon a series of canvas tents set up next to one another. Several wagons rolled in. Small groups gathered around fire pits. The setup reminded her of the group she and Alex had encountered, yet bigger.

"How many people do they expect to attend?" Sarah's backside was sore from sitting behind the saddle all day. Thankfully, traveling by horse didn't have the same effect riding in a wagon once did. Much faster too.

Will glanced at her and shrugged. "A few hundred, possibly more."

Enough that it would be impossible to find Alex if he came.

"What happens at these revivals?"

"We sing, pray, people speak and share their testimony, confess sins."

She frowned. "A church service?"

"Yes, but bigger. It's an opportunity for a larger community of believers to share their faith with others. Lives are changed. Testimonies shared. Many come to know the Lord at these events. I've been looking forward to participating in one since I started seminary."

Sarah gasped and squeezed Will's stomach. "Are you speaking?"

He nodded. "That's why I was in a rush."

Her heart faltered. How she missed Alex's "aye." She frowned. This was not the time to focus on what she lost. "I'm sorry, Will. I didn't mean to cause you so much trouble."

He moved the reins to his right hand and placed his left one on her hand. "I know you are. I'm sorry too. For not being there for you when you needed me. Especially when you lost Michael and then Ma. I had a short timeframe to get ordained so I could return to Washton before Pastor Kenneth left. Otherwise, the position wouldn't be available. I was here so I could be back home with you later. I should've realized—"

"No." Sarah shook her head. "Don't blame yourself. It's in the past. And I realize we had different circumstances influencing our decisions. I was only thinking of myself when I left."

"Well, no one else was, so you needed to. I'll talk with Luke when I get back to Washton. Try to explain to him. His ego is bruised, but he's not one to hold on to things. His life has changed a lot, too, with the loss of his parents, just as ours did for us. Life isn't easy. It's why we need Jesus."

Will's words echoed in her mind. Yes, her awareness of God had increased, and Alex had taught her how to pray and talk with Him. Alex had a strong faith. A faith she wanted too. This revival might be exactly what she needed.

"Thank you." She squeezed his back, held back tears from leaking out. Why did life have to be so hard? Why did tragedy strike? But even though she'd endured horrible circumstances, she'd survived. Lived to become a grown woman. Was this life the way God intended? Was there more? Maybe she and Will could talk about it later. She had questions she hoped he could answer.

He slowed his horse to a walk.

She lifted her head.

They had arrived.

Her mouth went dry. She had no idea what to expect.

Will dismounted, then reached for her. "I'm excited to introduce you to some of my new friends." He frowned. "I'm not sure how to explain where you came from."

She bit her lip. Her actions sure had a ripple effect she hadn't anticipated. "Did they know you were looking for me?"

He shook his head. "No. I asked for a leave right after I got the letter from Luke but didn't explain why. I decided to head toward Washton and see if I could intersect with you. I'd only passed two towns before stopping in Fairfield. God helped me find you."

"Then why don't we say I wanted to attend, so you picked me up and brought me here? It's not lying. I *am* interested in attending."

"All right." His eyes bored into hers. "Is it the truth? Alex didn't hurt you?"

"No, Will. If anything, he took better care of me than you would've."

He smirked. "That's saying something, because I take pretty good care of you."

She wanted to hug him again and hold on for a long time, but they were in the open. Instead, she squeezed his hand. "I've really missed you, brother."

He squeezed her hand back. "I've missed you too." He dropped her hand and unhooked his bedroll from the side of the saddle. We need to figure out where you will sleep tonight."

"Would it be okay to stay in your tent? I don't know anyone else."

"A pastor with a beautiful young woman who is not his wife sleeping in his tent? Yes, that will make a good impression with everyone." He wiggled his eyebrows.

Sarah had missed this teasing side of Will. "I'm your sister."

"Yes, you are." He nestled his arm around her shoulder and hugged her close.

Warmth spread through her. How did she think he didn't care about her. "What time does this start tomorrow?"

"Ten o'clock." He put his hand on the small of her back and

gently guided her forward. "Let's figure out some things. It's been a very long day for both of us."

Sarah pasted on a smile as they weaved through the grounds. They selected a tent and found supplies. As they settled in for the night, memories of campfire conversations with Alex filtered through her mind. Would he come? Would she see him again?

Did she even want to?

Eighteen

Early the next morning Alex broke camp and readied Bear for a few hours of travel. The horse nudged his shoulder. "I miss her, too, Bear. Aye, I do."

Bear didn't answer back, which left Alex unfulfilled in the conversation.

"It feels good to say the words out loud, though. Do you think she feels the same?" With no reply, Alex climbed onto the bench seat and flicked the reins.

The previous night Alex had pulled the wagon under a group of cottonwood trees. Even though he wanted to continue on, the darkness made it difficult to see the ruts in the road, and it was unsafe to keep going. Travel during the day was brutal and lonely. Nighttime was worse. He went through the motions to set up camp. Decided not to cook dinner over the campfire and ate the apple and jerky he had on hand instead. The glow from the fire provided the light he needed to reread the letters he'd received.

The strangest part? The tightness that had been in his chest for years was gone. He sorted through his emotions to figure out why. The answer eluded him. All he knew was he had wanted to follow where God led. And God had led him here, so how did the events in Scotland impact him now?

When he laid on his bedroll, the stars twinkled overhead, and he imagined God waiting for Alex to talk with Him. *God, I know you're the one in control. Many times we can't see your plan until we've gone through everything. Help me move out of the way so your plan for me is clear. Show me, Lord, what I'm supposed to do. I pray for my parents, and Rebecca and her family, and what happens next for all of them. Let this not become a lasting scandal. I pray for Sarah and her brother, Will, wherever they are. That they're safe and mending their relationship. Thank you, Lord, for loving me.*

The peace in Alex's heart as he fell asleep stayed with him through the morning. A few hours later, he drove through the small town of Bridgeport. The smaller town reminded him of the conversation he had with Sarah, and his heart thumped. He continued along the route outside of town, and when he rounded the last hill, a massive tent city came into view. He drove into the field full of wagons, unhitched Bear, and led him to the horse paddock.

Voices, some with unfamiliar accents, floated in the air. His heart leapt. He was ready to spend this time with others in worship and prayer. He prayed as he headed toward a group gathering near a makeshift table. *I'm here, God. Open my heart to what you need to teach me today. Even if it means I need to let go of my feelings for Sarah.*

* * *

THE RUSTLING of blankets stirred Sarah awake. Low light filtered through the canvas tent as dawn appeared. Through sleep-heavy eyes, she saw Will kneel and bow his head, lips moving soundlessly in prayer. The way he sat with his shoulders squared and hands steady reminded her of Pa. Memories of when they were young and their parents were still alive flooded her mind. Now older, she realized the security and hope she had felt was not from her family but from the Lord. Her brother seemed to never forget that, but she had.

Will raised his head and caught her watching him. "Do I have something on my face?"

She laughed, remembering the game they used to play. "Yep. Two eyes, a nose, and a mouth."

He smiled, love showing in his eyes.

She gave a half-hearted smile. "Will, I have to admit something. I ... I stopped praying after Michael passed. I bowed my head at the table. Went through the motions. But my heart wasn't in it. And I just realized this truth over the past week. I can pray any time. In my head with my eyes open or with them closed. While I'm moving and while I'm still. God just wants us to talk with him. I never grasped that before. Is that what you do?"

He nodded. "I think it's something we all have to figure out on our own. My prayer life wasn't always the best either. At school I studied God's word. Incorporated it into my prayers. Praying is a practice everyone needs to put into motion. You have to work at it. It doesn't happen automatically. And you have to keep at it."

Sarah looked away. "Life got challenging after you left. From sunup to sundown, we were busy. Death lurked everywhere. At first Luke and I trusted things would get better.

But they didn't. Even Uncle Jimmy kept to himself whenever there was a free moment."

"He was probably praying." Will shifted his body into a sitting position.

She nodded. "I agree. But at the time I didn't understand. My anger, or fear, or whatever took control. I knew something was off, but I didn't know what. I was suffocating." She pulled on a piece of grass and it came up in her hand.

"How did you figure this out?"

"Alex ..." She looked at her brother when he made a noise. The expression on his face was comical. "I know you don't trust him. But he's strong with the Lord. He encouraged me to talk to God and gave me the space to do it on my terms. He helped me figure some things out through his example."

Will pressed his lips together, but didn't say anything.

"I'm meant to be here. I feel closer to God."

He nodded, then smiled. "I'm happy to hear that."

She grabbed his arm. "It's more than that, though. I don't know how to explain it. When the men from the wagon train helped us with the broken wheel, I showed kindness to a woman and her children. I served, and amongst their sorrow, I was a light for them, even if for a moment. That's what Alex does every day. I thought he was a mere peddler who sold wares and had the freedom to travel anywhere he wanted, but God has him on a path to help people. And I want to do that too."

"You can help me back in Washton in the church. God knows I can't do it by myself."

"You don't understand. What happens when you find a wife? Where does that leave me? Besides Luke, who else in Washton would you see as my husband?"

Will opened his mouth and paused. "Um. Well, there's ..."

The concentration on his face would've made her laugh if the topic wasn't so serious.

"Even though there isn't anyone coming to mind right now, there has to be someone. There were always more men than women in Washton."

"But would you want any of them as a brother-in-law?"

He narrowed his eyes. "You know who I would like to have as my brother-in-law, but you don't see him in that way."

She grinned. "It would be like me marrying you."

His mouth fell open.

"See what I mean? Admit it. You can't name anyone." If she wasn't so happy to be right, sadness would encroach that her brother hadn't considered how few potential suitors were available in Washton.

His face lit up as if he had the correct answer. It scared her a bit, wondering where his mind went off to. "Forget Washton."

She let out the breath she held.

"I'll introduce you to a friend I went to seminary with. Nice fella. Should hold your fancy."

She shook her head. "You know nothing about romantic love."

"Who says there needs to be romance? You just need someone who will treat you well and take care of you. Matthew would be perfect for you."

"Will." Sarah raised her voice. "You're not listening to me."

"What? You said you wanted to help people. Being a pastor's wife is the best way to do that."

"I don't want to settle down in one community as a pastor's wife."

They stared at each other as her comment sunk in. Will's head snapped back as if she'd slapped him.

She placed her hand on his. "There's nothing wrong with being a pastor's wife."

He pulled his hand from hers. "Obviously you think there is." Only with her, would he show his hurt.

She hesitated. Standing up for herself was still something she wasn't used to doing. But if she wanted her brother to see her in a different light, she had to find a way to show him. "It's not the right role for *me*." She paused, hoping he understood. "I know you mean well, but that's not the life I want. It wouldn't feel right. Not for me. I think God has other plans for who I'm to marry." Alex came to mind, but she shook it off. He wasn't who God intended for her either.

Will's agitation came through in his words. "Well, you can't go traipsing around by yourself. Who would let you travel with them if you weren't married? I need to know you're settled somewhere, sis. I love you. I want to know who will be looking after you if I can't."

Sarah hugged him. A tear fell. He meant well, and for that her heart was grateful. But she'd learned a thing or two over the past few days. About herself and her brother. They weren't going to fix in one conversation. But maybe there was room for them to find understanding in prayer. "We aren't going to solve this today. How about we pray about it and then discuss it further after the revival."

His face softened, and he nodded. "You're right. I need to get ready. I think my nerves are affecting my mind a bit. Will you sit with me when it all starts?"

She reached over and hugged him. "I'd be proud to."

A short time later, Sarah exited the tent and found Will waiting for her. How had he managed to find fresh clothes close to her size? After sleeping and riding in the same dress for several days, she was relieved to make herself presentable. Especially if she was to sit next to Will before he spoke at the start of the event. They walked to the main tent, where he escorted her to the front row.

He rose after his introduction and stood at the podium with a calm and comfortable stance. Sarah had never heard her brother so passionate, nor heard a message presented in such a personal way. Her heart filled. He had grown while he'd been gone and would do well leading their church back home.

After his message, she excused herself and headed to the food tent to volunteer. She had heard they needed help and the desire to serve urged her to seek out an opportunity to do so.

An older lady around the age her mother would've been intercepted her as she entered. "Hello. I'm Ellie."

"Hi. Ellie. I'm Sarah. Do you need help with anything?"

"Praise the Lord. Do we ever." She leaned closer. "I prayed for help, and in you came." She reached for Sarah's hand. "Come with me, I know just the thing for you to do."

Sarah allowed herself to be led. As they wandered by the other women, Sarah noticed the abundant amount of food being prepared. They were expecting a lot of people throughout the day.

Ellie stopped at the end of a table. "Sarah, this is Alma. Alma, this is Sarah. She's going to help you with the bread."

Bread. Sarah knew how to do this. She pulled up her sleeves and assessed the space in front of her. Alma's apron was covered in flour. Sarah glanced at her borrowed dress and hesitated.

Alma handed her a fresh apron.

"Oh, thank you." She pulled the garment over her clothes.

Alma smiled. "You know what to do?"

Sarah nodded. "Yes, I've baked lots of bread back home. Do you have fresh dough for me to work with?"

Alma handed her the sticky dough from her station.

Sarah placed it in front of her and got right to work. There was little chatter amongst the women as they prepared the food, yet a sense of awe filled the space. As if they were preparing a feast for the Lord. Sarah's body vibrated with renewed energy, thankful to be a part of something special.

An hour flew by, and her arms and back ached from shaping several batches of bread, but she didn't complain. It felt good to be useful. On to her last set, her mind wandered. Back to Alex and their discussions. What he shared and didn't share. She now understood why he never brought up his family or his dreams. He'd been betrothed to someone else the entire time. As much as her heart hurt, she couldn't stop thinking about him.

Sarah's palm dug into the center of the dough, and she folded it over.

A tap on her arm startled her. "Yes?"

Alma pointed to the mound in her hands. "I think it's ready to be put in the basket."

Sarah poked her finger into the tight, stiff ball she'd overworked. It was indeed ready. "Sorry. I got distracted."

The woman smiled, revealing a missing tooth. "Lots on your mind, dear?"

Sarah blew out a breath. "Is it that obvious?"

"Only to those of us who understand. We all have thoughts and feelings we need to sort through. Do you want to talk about it?"

"Um." She bit her lip. Fear of being called foolish for falling for a man so quickly prevented her from admitting her feelings.

"It's not a problem to share, but I will not push you. Men can create a lot of worry for us women. We have to stick together." Alma picked up multiple baskets.

Sarah picked up the rest. "It's silly. I shouldn't feel this way."

"Oh, precious. Don't berate yourself. When your heart's

involved, it's not silly at all. What you feel is real. Sometimes we can't control the feelings, but we can ask the Lord to help guide our actions. You have done this, yes?"

Sarah cast her gaze down. What type of believer was she for not praying for God to help her with this?

"I can see you want to chastise yourself. Don't. Let's finish up the risen loaves and carry the baskets over to the coals. We can step outside and cool off while we talk some more." She headed the way she indicated.

Sarah followed, appreciating the woman's caring nature. With no mother around, nor sisters old enough to understand, she welcomed the woman's counsel. They found a log to sit on far enough away from prying ears, and Sarah poured out her heart.

The woman grabbed Sarah's hands. "You have found yourself a good man. I don't think you should give up."

Sarah couldn't see what Alma did. "What do you mean? He has to marry someone else."

Alma squeezed her hands once more, then shrugged. "Sometimes the unknown and waiting for an answer from the Lord is so difficult, isn't it?"

Sarah studied their clasped hands. "I don't know what I'm supposed to do."

"Then don't try to figure it all out at once, child. Trust in the Lord with all your heart."

Sarah knew the verse Alma mentioned, had heard it many times. But sitting here, in this place with the comforting scent of oak enveloping her and the quiet assurance in Alma's voice, the words felt different. More personal.

She exhaled slowly. "I guess I haven't been doing much trusting lately."

Alma patted her shoulder. "Then maybe it's time to start."

Nineteen

The event was in full swing when Alex arrived. The midday break gave him a chance to introduce himself and confirm his speaking time. But restlessness gnawed at him. He scanned the camp. A group of men stood in a circle, heads bowed in prayer.

When they finished, one turned around and noticed him. "Hi. Welcome. I'm Matthew."

"Alex Smith." He reached out his hand as his false last name tasted sour in his mouth.

Matthew grabbed his hand and shook it eagerly. "Alex, great to meet you. I heard you were coming today. Are you all set to speak this afternoon?"

Alex took a deep breath and asked the Lord for confidence. "Aye."

"Great." Matthew peered over Alex's shoulder. "Will," he shouted. "Come here. There's someone I want you to meet."

Alex turned and caught Sarah's brother with his mouth gaped open.

He froze.

Matthew looked back and forth at the pair. "Do you two know each other? Will, this is Alex. He's going to be speaking today and sharing his testimony."

Will walked over to where Alex and Matthew stood.

Alex held out his hand, hoping Will would not cause a scene.

"Hi, Alex." Will slowly reached out and shook his hand, confusion etched on his face. "Nice to meet you."

Someone called for Matthew from afar.

"I need to go answer their question. I look forward to your talk, Alex. Will, see you later." He ran off.

Will's brow furrowed as he studied Alex. "Huh." He crossed his arms, eyes narrowed. "Didn't expect that."

Alex braced himself. "Expect what?"

"You. Standing here. Talking about faith. But you must not fully trust the Lord because you're using a false name.

Alex searched for the words to explain. "As I said earlier, I needed others to see me as an ordinary person, not be enticed by my background and title. I want to make a difference by showing God's love. Not by relying on a name tied to wealth and influence."

Will nodded. "I guess I can understand that."

"Thank you. I really mean no harm." Before he had a chance to ask about Sarah, several men came over and introduced themselves.

They discussed what he would be speaking about, and the men walked away, Will among with them.

Alex dashed after him. "Will, wait up."

Will stopped but didn't turn around.

"Is Sarah with ye?"

Will pivoted and studied him.

"Please, I need to know. Is she okay? I'd like to see her again."

"Why? Why toy with her emotions? She cares for you."

Alex's heart tumbled at the confirmation.

"But you told us yourself that you can't offer for her. What purpose would you have in seeing her?"

Alex's fumbled with his coat pocket. "I've received some news. In the letters."

Will placed his hands on his hips. "Yeah, what about them?"

"They were from my family and my betrothed." He pinned Will down with all the sincerity he could muster. "She's called our betrothal off. Publicly. And my family acknowledged the action. There is no more commitment. I am free to marry whomever I choose."

Will's face went pale. "Why are you telling me this?"

Alex pulled off his hat and held it by his chest. "You're Sarah's brother. You're responsible for her, aye. I want to ask yer permission to marry her."

Alex waited by the wooden platform. A large group of people sat on crates, blankets, and wooden benches under the tent, all eyes on Matthew, who was making Alex's introduction. He scanned the audience for a familiar face, but didn't see her. He ran a finger under his tight collar. His stomach twisted with anticipation. But it wasn't all due to sharing his testimony.

Now his nerves were a different sort.

After much discussion with Will, he had agreed for Alex to

marry his sister. But he hadn't seen her today. Will thought she was in the food tent, but when they went inside, there was no sign of her. Alex gave her description to the woman in charge, Ellie, who'd said she'd been there, but no one knew where she'd gone. He waited for a while, anxious to talk with her, but the chance never came.

Now he had to speak, knowing she believed he would marry someone else. He just hoped he didn't shout it out for everyone to hear. He wanted to keep the moment quiet and special between the two of them. Alex made Will promise not to say anything to her before he could talk with her himself.

"I now introduce Alex Smith." Matthew turned toward Alex and clapped his hands, welcoming him to the platform.

Polite applause carried Alex to the podium. *God, give me the words to say right now.*

"Good evening and welcome. Like so many of you, my life has been full of ups and downs. There have been moments when I've asked myself, "Is this all?" But as I've grown closer to the Lord, I know without a doubt he loves me and he's there for me. He has a plan for each of us." He laughed. "And sometimes he redirects us by turning our plans upside down to get our attention."

A calmness overcame Alex as he shared the message God had urged him to share. This was important and he wanted to get it right. The words flowed out of him. Near the end, as he turned to the side, a swatch of blue caught his attention and he paused. Sarah.

She stared at him. A smile crossed her lips, and Alex's heart filled with encouragement. He refocused on the crowd before him as he reached a pinnacle of his message.

"Not long ago, I thought my future was set. Years of obligations and a promise I had no right to break. Unchangeable. But God." Alex glanced up before continuing.

"He has a way of undoing the plans we make to reveal His perfect plan." It took everything within him to not let his gaze wander back to Sarah. He hoped she understood what he was trying to say.

"I get to make a new covenant now. One that's my heart's desire. A lifetime of promises. A forever vow full of love. And through this, I've learned that God makes promises too. He promises to always be there for us, even when we can't feel his presence. He promises an eternal life with him if we believe and accept his love. He promises to never leave us or forsake us, no matter if we get distracted or forget to pray.

"What do these assurances mean to me? Everything. I am not alone. God is bigger than I am, and I have someone to bring my burdens to. The Bible tells us in Psalm 55:16, 'As for me, I will call upon God; and the Lord shall save me.' Life never goes the way we think it should. But if we keep an open mind, we can see where the Lord is leading us. We can find joy and peace no matter where we are. I ask all of you to join me in prayer."

Alex prayed from his heart. For those in attendance and their families. Those sick and hurting. And the rest of the event. Then he turned, walked off the stage, and headed straight for Sarah. She stood with her hands clasped in front of her and she was biting her lip. He reached for her hand, lifted it to his lips and kissed her knuckles. "I am so happy to see you again."

A tentative smile crossed her face. Her timidness was unusual, but at least she didn't pull her hand away. That meant something, right?

"Let's take a walk." He tucked her hand into his elbow and strode away from the crowd. He focused on what he wanted to say to her. He didn't want to muck this up.

She bit her lip. Squeezed his arm. "Um. Were you talking to me while you were up there?"

Aye, she'd heard. Now to say the rest, these words for her ears only.

* * *

ALEX HOLDING her hand caused Sarah's stomach to do a crazy flip-flop.

Alex smiled at her, his eyes glistening. "Aye, I had hoped ye were listening."

She would have liked a more direct answer.

He walked her to a small group of trees and asked her to sit on the same log where she had her discussion with Alma earlier. At this point he could've asked her to jump up and down, and she would've done so without question. She was thankful God designed people to breathe without thinking, or she wouldn't be able to find any air.

"Sarah, I need to tell ye my entire story. I'm sorry I didn't explain sooner. I never meant to hide my life from ye. I didn't want to. But I'm not who I was when I first arrived five years ago. I'm Alex Smith, even though on paper I'm still Alex Sinclair."

"You don't have to explain anything to me. I understand. And I trust you." She emphasized her last words so he understood how important he was to her.

He nodded. "Thank you for yer belief in me. Ye knew I received news from home in Fairfield. After ye and yer brother left, I received another letter. My betrothed publicly declared herself … unbetrothed." His grin turned a little sheepish.

"Can she do that?" Sarah didn't understand anything about the rules of his country or nobility.

"Aye. She can and she did. The lady can break the contract, but not the man. It tarnished my family's reputation a bit, but it doesn't really change anything. But that's not the reason I tell ye this."

Would he say what she hoped he would? Her heart wanted to burst out of her chest as she waited for him to continue.

He reached for her hands again. "Sarah, I care for ye. But I couldn't tell or show ye in any way. It wouldn't have been fair to ye or to me when I was unable to act on my feelings. Honor and promise are important to me. When I make a commitment, I keep it." He paused. "Your stubbornness and spunkiness are quite a combination. Something I admire."

Her mouth opened, but she couldn't find her voice.

He shook her hands to get her attention. "I'm not saying this right." He paused and got down on one knee. "Sarah, I love you. I think it started the first night ye were determined to go with me. Intent on sitting on the bench seat and suffering through motion sickness every mile we traveled. I am amazed by ye. Ye are special and one of a kind. And I don't want to *ever* watch ye walk away from me again like ye did yesterday. I don't have much to offer ye, and I don't know what the future holds. But I love the Lord, and I love ye, and together the three of us will weather any storm. Will ye be my wife? Would ye spend the rest of yer life with me?" A light hue of pink appeared on his cheeks as he paused and searched her face.

He cared for her. Wanted to be with her. All she had to do was answer him.

He reached up and touched her cheek.

His calloused fingers against her skin caused a flushing sensation throughout her body. Tears pricked her eyes, her pounding heart ready to leap into his loving hands. Could she do this? Could she trust in what she felt, in what God had placed before her?

Twenty

My heart is grateful for such a precious gift. My Sarah. This wasn't the plan I had in mind when I came to this rugged land, but it was God's plan all along. And it turned out more beautiful than I could have imagined.

—From the journal of Alex Sinclair

Alex's heart beat hard in his chest. His ears rang as well, so he worried he'd miss her answer.

She was taking an awful long time to respond.

He frowned. Maybe she didn't feel the same way as he. Had he misinterpreted somehow? No matter. He still would've said those things. He wanted her to know everything. And he wanted to hear from her.

"Sarah ... Sarah, honey, are ye okay?"

Her hands grew cold, and her face lost its color. She tipped toward the ground, and he caught her before she hit the grass. She lay limp in his arms. "Sarah?" No response. He scooped her up and carried her to the covered tent where the water jugs were. A lady glanced up and saw him coming. She hurried to open the tent flap and ushered him inside. Then quickly escorted him out.

He stood there, staring at the canvas material, wishing he could see inside. What just happened? One minute he was declaring himself. And the next she'd crumpled to the floor.

* * *

SOMETHING COLD PRESSED on Sarah's forehead, and she moved her head back and forth. Her eyes wouldn't open, but she couldn't understand why. Pressure on her hand came next. Then she heard voices, but she couldn't make out the words.

The urge to sit up was met with pressure on her shoulder. "Shh. It's okay. Lay still and wait a moment."

She moved her head back and forth some more, and a nauseated feeling overcame her. She placed her hand on her stomach. "I don't feel so well."

"You gave us all quite a scare." Alma's voice floated above her. "Have you had much water to drink today? I think you may have a case of dehydration. Or a severe headache from all the stress you've been under. Here, take a sip."

Sarah opened her eyes to find a familiar face smiling at her. Alma helped her sit up and sip from the ladle a few times. Once the older woman was satisfied she'd had enough to drink, she placed a fresh cloth on Sarah's head.

She closed her eyes again. What happened? Wait. Alex had proposed. Alex. Where was he?

"Alex." she whispered. A commotion outside the tent had her lifting her head too fast. She closed her eyes and waited for the dizziness to subside.

"Would you please let me in to see her?"

It was his voice. She'd recognize it anywhere.

"I can't. Not without permission. What relation do you have to her, sir?"

She heard him hesitate. "I ... I'm ... I'm her fiancé." Bless the man. He asked her to marry him, and she hadn't answered him yet. The doubt in his voice said as much. His strong, nothing-ever-phases-me demeanor was missing. All because he didn't know if she would say yes.

"Alex," she called out.

Alma patted her shoulder. "What's that, dearie?"

"Alex." She locked eyes with the woman, pleading for her understanding.

"Is the gentleman out there your man? The one we discussed earlier?" A knowing smile beamed down at her.

She winced when she nodded but smiled anyway. She liked the sound of "your man." "Yes," she whispered.

"Would you like him to come in?" Alma asked. "I think I already know your answer."

Sarah smiled bigger. "Yes, please."

"Hold on. I'll see what I can do." Alma left her side and exited the tent.

Murmurs came from outside, but she couldn't make out the words. Then the tent flaps flew back and a man stood in the opening, sunlight glinting around him like a halo. Her man. Her hero. She raised her hand to him.

He rushed to her side and clutched it. "Sarah. Are ye okay? Ye gave me such a fright."

By this time, her senses were in place and she felt much better. "Help me sit up."

"Careful." He put his arm around her back for support.

Their faces were so close she could feel his warm breath on

her cheek. She looked into his crystal-blue eyes and saw a mix of concern and love. Her heart melted.

He brushed a loose hair off her face.

She felt cherished and loved. "I never answered you."

A flicker in his eyes showed the self-doubt hidden behind. "Yes, my love."

"Yes," she whispered.

"Whit?"

She laughed. She would never tire of hearing his accent. "Yes, yes, yes. Yes, I'll marry you. Yes, I'll go wherever you go. Yes, I will be your bride forever."

He closed his eyes and hugged her to him.

She wrapped her arms around his back.

Their breathing became one.

He pulled back, bent down, and pressed his lips to hers. Warm, soft, and so gentle, Sarah forgot about everything around them. After a few minutes, they each pulled back. Her ears warmed. He smiled at her in a way she would never tire of.

Full of awe, she studied his face. Even when she had no plan at all, God showed her the way. Because she knew without a doubt, God had directed her into the arms of this man. Alex was God's plan for her all along.

That evening, Alex and Sarah stood facing each other in front of Will. Next to Sarah stood Alma and Ellie, while Matthew stood beside Alex.

Will cleared his throat. "Alex. Repeat after me. I, Alex, uh Smith."

Alex stared into Sarah's eyes. "I, Alexander George Sinclair."

Will glanced up from his book and smiled. He prompted Alex with the rest of the wedding vows.

"Take thee, Sarah, to be my lawful wedded wife. To have

and to hold, from this day forward, for better, for worse, for richer, for poorer, in sickness and in health. To love and cherish, until death do us part."

When Alex was done, Will faced Sarah.

A tear escaped down her cheek and into her smile as her brother walked her through her own vows. "I, Sarah Anne Baker, take thee, Alexander, to be my lawful wedded husband. To have and to hold, from this day forward, for better, for worse, for richer, for poorer, in sickness and in health. To love, cherish and obey, until death do us part."

With no rings to exchange, Alex held up his Bible and handed it to Sarah. "We share God's word. Together. Always." She gently accepted the offered gift and searched his face. "I don't have one to give you."

"Ahem." Will cleared his throat. "I have you covered, Sarah."

She glanced at her brother. Sure enough, he held out a book. "I had planned to give this to you anyway. It's our family Bible, and it's yours to do with as you please." He placed the book in her other hand and she passed it to Alex. "We share God's word. Together. Always."

Once that was done, Will studied the two of them. His eyes shone. "Your two hearts have been joined as one in holy matrimony. By the power vested in me by the state of California, I now pronounce you husband and wife." He swallowed as he turned to Alex. "You may kiss your bride."

The smile on Alex's face grew as he regarded her. He leaned down, and she closed her eyes. His warm lips pressed against hers and released them too soon. When she opened her eyes, his danced with pleasure. And a promise of more.

Tomorrow she would leave with her husband. To travel and serve together, wherever the Lord would lead them. When

Sarah left Washton, she never expected to marry the man. That was not her intention. She only wanted to escape. And now she'd found her life partner. And her brother performed the ceremony.

It was as if the best-laid out plan had fallen into place.

And the best part was yet to come.

Thank you!

Thank you for reading *No Plan At All*

I hope you enjoyed Sarah and Alex's story. It would mean so much if you would take a quick minute to leave a review.

(https://scrivenings.link/noplanatall)

It doesn't have to be long. Just a sentence or two telling what you liked about the book (but no spoilers, please).

When writing a historical novel, there are specific events a writer wants to include. For my story to take place when it did, I had to take a bit of liberty with the timeline on some of these events to fit my fictional story.

I had fun digging into the area Alex and Sarah traveled. There were several surprising things I learned in my research I tried to incorporate into my story. And a few others I will write about in future blog posts.

The most interesting fact was learning the Pony Express had to use this route a few times when they missed the final stop at the Sacramento train station. I found a detailed accounting of the trail blazened by these riders in order to deliver the mail in time. Of course, this all changed once the train tracks were laid. The towns Alex and Sarah visited changed because of the railroad as well, including the offical names of the towns that stand today.

I researched several maps from the 1870's which listed town names inconsistently, so I had to decide on which ones to use. If you are from the area and refer to a town differently, I apologize in advance. I was able to find references to why they changed to what they are now, but none which explained the differences between maps.

Since I grew up in this area, it was fun to explore in more detail. I love writing about the research I've uncovered on my blog. Be sure to follow my blog posts on GoodReads and on Facebook, my website, www.denisemcolby.com and other social media to learn more.

Acknowledgments

Thank *you*, dear reader, for going along on this adventure with me and reading this book. I hope you enjoyed Sarah and Alex's story. My stories couldn't be written without readers, and I appreciate every single one of you.

To my husband Ken and to my kids, who have patiently endured discussions of writing struggles, book topics, and fictional characters. And a special shoutout to my son Kyle, for creating a great map of the journey Alex and Sarah take (as well as the town of Washton's map, Bert, and my schoolhouse logo).

To all my family and friends who have encouraged me by purchasing and reading my books, sending me texts and pictures, asking interesting questions about my stories. I love that you have chosen to go along this adventure with me.

I've dedicated this story to my critique partners Kimberly Keagan, Marie Wells Coutu, and Christina Rich. Their support and encouragement as I write each story has been the best gift. I love our group and our interactions with each other. I highly recommend their stories to my readers as well.

Thank you also to all my other writer friends. I belong to several groups and the friendships I have made are special. I can't list everyone here because the list is long, but I did want to say thank you. I've learned and grown as a writer because of you, and I love that I now get to share promotions and book launches with all of you.

A special shout-out to my publisher Scrivenings Press, my editors Ann Harrison and Suzie Waltner.

Last, but certainly not least, I thank God for providing the opportunity to write this story and for it to be published. Writing a novel is not easy. And he has provided the people, the tools, and the story ideas to help me make this a reality. To Him be the glory.

About the Author

Passionate about all types of stories—whether they are from songs, theatre, movies, or novels—Denise M. Colby loves history and constantly finds herself contemplating how it was to live in the 1800s.

An avid journal writer, Denise usually can be found with a pen and notepad whenever she's reading God's word. Each year, Denise chooses a word to focus on. She shares her learnings about that word throughout the year on the two blogs she writes for.

A wife for thirty years and mother to three boys and daughter-in-love, Denise loves to read, watch movies with her family, sing 80s and musical songs, dance, and spend date nights with her husband.

Writing Historical Christian Romance novels combines her love of learning about history and reading. Visit Denise's website to sign up for her newsletter or connect with her on her social media. www.denisemcolby.com

When Plans Go Awry

Best-laid Plans—Book One

Olivia Carmichael escapes her past to be the next schoolmarm in the small ranching community of Washton, California. Her plan? Live a quiet spinster life, alone, never to depend on anyone ever again.

Luke Taylor selected a mail-order bride, a necessity to help raise his two younger sisters and the only way he knew to protect his heart. His plans don't include being responsible for the beautiful new schoolmarm, who threatens his resolve between his need to stay away and his need to be near to make sure she stays safe.

Along the way, neither feel much in control of their circumstances. Olivia's carefully laid-out plans are challenged at every turn, and Luke's mail-order bride is not what he expected. Will Luke and Olivia learn to trust God's plan for their lives?

Get your copy here:

https://scrivenings.link/whenplansgoawry

* * *

A Slight Change of Plans

Best-laid Plans—Book Two

She believes she doesn't matter

Jenny Millard's hopes for security and stability as a schoolmarm out west are dashed when her schoolhouse closes, and no positions are available nearby. With only enough money for a one-way train fare, Jenny heads to her friend's home, uncertain of her next step.

His scars have made him an unlovable outcast

Newcomer Ren Lyman prefers to keep to himself, hiding in the back of the blacksmith shop to avoid the stares at the scars left by a childhood accident. When he comes across a lost stranger, he's surprised when she doesn't recoil at his appearance and even more so at his eagerness to assist her.

As Jenny settles into the welcoming but small town of Washton, she can't help but come across Ren, especially since his daily constitutional takes him along the same path. It doesn't take long for them to form a connection that breaks down the walls erected by years of hurt. But when strange occurrences unsettle the townspeople, it seems their chance at happiness might be at risk.

Will Jenny and Ren discover that they're enough—for God ... and each other?

Get your copy here:

https://scrivenings.link/aslightchangeofplans

* * *

Stay up-to-date on your favorite books and authors with our free e-newsletters.

ScriveningsPress.com